"I can't use the excuse of sun in my eyes. I'll admit I was staring."

He stated the offhand compliment with an intimate kind of amusement that made Carole blush. She hadn't blushed in years. She thought she'd forgotten how.

"And you are...?"

"I'm sorry. I'm still excited about my daughter's win. Carole Jacks," she said, forcing herself to smile pleasantly when she wanted to gawk at the blue-green eyes of the stranger like a sixteen-year-old.

His expression changed from intimate interest to disbelief in a flash. Seconds later he blinked and schooled his features into a painfully benign mask. "You... I don't suppose you have another relative by the same name. A mother or aunt, perhaps?"

This book is lovingly dedicated
to Rochelle Lynn Dove and her family.

I would like to thank Joan Bompane for her helpful
input and all the dedicated health personnel who
are warring with childhood cancer.

SIX MONTHS
TO LIVE

CONTENTS

RL: 6.0 AGES 012 and UP

DAWN ROCHELLE: FOUR NOVELS
A Bantam Book / published by arrangement with
Willowisp Press

July 2000

Text copyright © 2000 by Lurlene McDaniel
Cover art copyright © 2000 by Ericka O'Rourke

Visit us on the Web! www.randomhouse.com/teens

Educators and librarians, for a variety of teaching tools, visit us at
www.randomhouse.com/teachers

Check out Lurlene McDaniel's Web site! www.lurlenemcdaniel.com

Published simultaneously in the United States and Canada

BANTAM BOOKS is an imprint of Random House Children's Books, a division of
Random House, Inc. BANTAM BOOKS and the rooster colophon are registered
trademarks of Random House, Inc. Bantam Books, 1540 Broadway, New York,
New York 10036.

PRINTED IN THE UNITED STATES OF AMERICA

OPM 10 9 8 7 6

Lurlene McDaniel

DAWN ROCHELLE

Four Novels

BANTAM BOOKS
NEW YORK • TORONTO • LONDON • SYDNEY • AUCKLAND

From *So Much to Live For*

"Can I speak to Dawn, please?" The girl's voice on the other end of the receiver sounded quivery and familiar.

"This is Dawn. Who's this?"

"I—It's me—Marlee Hodges."

For no reason, Dawn's heart skipped a beat. "Hi. How are you? Is everything all right?"

"No." Marlee's voice wavered.

Dawn clutched the receiver so tightly that her fingers hurt. "What's wrong?"

"I'm back in the hospital and I'm scared. Please, come see me, Dawn. Please."

From *No Time to Cry*

Dawn staggered to the bathroom, convinced that a warm shower would make her feel better. But when she shed her nightgown and looked into the mirror, her heart wedged in her throat. A fine red rash covered her arms and torso. She started shaking so violently that she had to grab hold of the sink for support.

Dawn knew what the rash meant. She'd read too many pamphlets and booklets following her transplant. A rash was often the very first sign of bone marrow rejection.

DAWN ROCHELLE
Four Novels

From *Six Months to Live*

"The preliminary tests are back," the elderly doctor said, his penetrating brown eyes grave with concern. "The tests point to cancer, specifically, acute lymphocytic leukemia. It's one of the most common forms of cancer among kids. A bone marrow aspiration will confirm the preliminary diagnosis." His voice sounded concerned, but final.

A kid! That's what I am, Dawn thought. She *was* a kid, just two months over her thirteenth birthday. . . .

From *I Want to Live*

"This is not a decision for you to make right now, Dawn," Dr. Sinclair said, breaking the heavy silence. "Go home and think about it. Discuss it. But don't take too long. We'll need to proceed as soon as possible if you decide in favor of the procedure."

"The odds," Rob said. "What are the odds of the transplant succeeding?"

The two doctors exchanged quick glances. "Without it, Dawn has a twenty percent chance of survival. With it, fifty-fifty."

(Continued on next page)

coming through the open windows, he needed to make sure he wasn't seeing a mirage. No, she was real.

Standing directly across the dusty arena was a woman who would make any man forget his parched throat. Blond hair, tied back in a low ponytail, escaped the black cowboy hat she wore. A white T-shirt left little to his imagination, molding to breasts that appeared just the right size. And that big silver belt buckle fastened around a waist that obviously hadn't eaten too many of "Ms. Carole's Cookies." He could tell she wasn't too tall, but in those tight blue jeans, her legs looked as if they went on forever.

She stepped onto the bottom rail of the fence, then folded her arms along the top and rested her chin. The position caused her to bend a little, curving her rear out just enough to send a stampede of wicked fantasies through Greg's imagination. Unfortunately, the pounding affected more than his mind. He propped one boot on the bottom rail and hoped no one noticed his new jeans were even tighter than before he'd fantasized about the blonde. Or worse yet, thought that he had a predilection for either tractors or cows.

She must be waiting for something...or someone. The thought of her watching one of those overposturing cowboys sent a jolt of adrenaline through his body. He gripped the top rail and vowed not to leap over the fence, no matter what she did or who she cheered for. He would not make a fool of himself over the blond cowgirl, not in front of the formidable Carole Jacks. Not when he was here on a mission to save his family's company from the unfortunate remarks of his hotheaded older brother, who just happened to be the former C.E.O. The man who'd publicly insulted the "food police" on national television not once, not twice, but the magic three times. And now he was "out" of Huntington Foods.

Greg tore his eyes away from the blonde when some official-looking people began filing into the arena. He forced himself to focus on his image of Carole Jacks, but none of the people standing there looked like America's favorite "cookie queen."

"And now for our final event, the Junior Steer Championship. After the grand champion is named, we'll have our annual auction this afternoon at two o'clock. The highest bid will help send one of these young people to college. Let's have a round of applause for these 4-H-ers who have raised these fine steers."

Before the applause ended, the cows—no, steers—entered the ring. They were led by a variety of kids, which obviously explained the "junior" part of the competition. Perhaps one of them was Ms. Carole's grandkid. Greg forced himself to scan the bleachers, but his gaze came back to the blonde. He couldn't stop looking at her, especially when she tensed, then waved at one of the kids entering the arena.

A brown-haired girl smiled back, then tugged on the rope leading her huge steer into the ring. The large black creature had big dark eyes and looked around calmly, as though it trusted the girl to lead it to victory.

Surely this ten-or eleven-year-old child wasn't the blond cowgirl's daughter. Greg looked between the alluring curves at the rail and the pixyish braids of the girl and couldn't reconcile the image. Still, the look of love on the face of his cowgirl seemed to confirm a strong relationship.

His cowgirl. Now that was a surprise. He'd never

developed such strong fantasies or compelling questions about a woman he had yet to meet.

As the competition progressed, he watched the steer, the child and the cowgirl. When the judges motioned for the little girl to lead the animal to the center of the ring along with four others, his cowgirl put her hands over her mouth and tensed even more.

Greg turned to the man with the battered soft drink can. Apparently he'd returned sometime during the steer judging. "Is it good that they're in the center of the arena?"

"Means they're in the final round," the man explained before spitting into the can.

Greg winced at the disgusting habit and turned his attention back to the ring. The judges circled the animals. One red-and-white steer stamped its foot. Another sidled away from the judge, nearly bumping the black animal held by the girl. She leaned close and spoke to her steer, rubbing his cheek with her fingers. He stood quietly, his feet even and steady.

"The big black one," Greg said, motioning toward the pair. "Is he doing okay?"

"Standing good and square."

"Do you think he might win?"

"Might." The man spat into his can again.

Greg turned his attention back to the girl again. She seemed to be blinking back some tears. Probably tears of happiness that she was a finalist and her steer was behaving so well.

In less than a minute the judges began handing out ribbons. A purple banner, two feet long at least, went to the little girl with the black steer. Greg applauded, a genuine smile surprising him as he watched her accept the congratulations of the judges.

When he looked at his cowgirl, though, he was surprised by the mix of emotions she seemed to be feeling. She smiled, but wiped tears from her eyes at the same time. Her heart seemed to be going out to the girl, and Greg's suspicions were confirmed that the brown-haired pixie was indeed her child.

The little girl hugged the big steer, burying her face in his slick, thick coat. She seemed to be holding on for dear life.

"She doesn't seem too happy to have won," Greg said out loud.

The man beside him nodded. "She got that steer from Billy Maddox over in Boerne when ever'body else said it weren't big enough. Look at it now."

"So she should be proud."

"I 'spect she is, but she's got to say goodbye to him now."

"Why? She won."

The man looked at him as though he was crazy. "What the hell do you think they do with the grand-champion steer?"

Greg searched his mind but couldn't come up with an answer. "Give it a ribbon, I suppose. Maybe she can show it somewhere else."

"None of these steers are going to the State Fair. That's a whole 'nother class of animal."

"So what do they do with them?"

The man spat into his can. "Auction 'em off." He nodded toward the tent. "Big Jim usually bids the highest."

"So what does Big Jim do with them?"

"Why, he has just about the finest barbecue you've ever seen for all his favorite customers over at Big Jim's Autorama on Highway 281."

As Greg watched in stunned silence, his cowgirl slipped between the rails of the fence and hurried to the little girl, who still had her face buried in the neck of the huge beast. Her thin shoulders shook, and Greg knew without a doubt that he couldn't let that pet steer end up on Big Jim's barbecue grill.

AS THEY WALKED out of the ring toward the barn, Carole could have kicked herself. She should have spent the extra money and bought a heifer instead of a steer. But she hadn't expected that runty calf to grow into the grand champion at the county show. The look on her daughter's face when she'd been handed the banner had nearly brought her to her knees, right there in the arena. Jenny had a soft heart, and darn it, Puff was a big old sweetheart—all twelve hundred pounds of him.

"We have a few hours, sweetie. What would you like to do?"

Jenny shrugged as if it didn't make any difference, but Carole could see her daughter's white-knuckled grip on Puff's halter. "I think I'll just hang around the barn. Put my stuff up."

Say goodbye to Puff, Carole felt like adding. She had always told her daughter that she could do or be anything she wanted, but that didn't mean life was always easy.

"I could bring you a snow cone or some cotton candy," Carole offered as she wrapped her arm around her ten-year-old's shoulders.

"Thanks, Mom, but I'm not hungry."

"We'll celebrate later, then."

Jenny nodded, but couldn't hide her sniff.

They stopped at their spot along the cattle rail. Carole hugged her arms around herself as Jenny attached the tie-down to Puff's halter. "Sure I can't get you anything? A cold drink?"

Jenny shrugged.

"Do you want to be alone?"

"Please," she said in a small voice.

"Okay, then. I'm going to get us a soft drink."

Carole took one more look at her little girl before turning and walking down the long corridor, out of the stock barn. Telling herself that this was an important lesson, that Jenny would feel proud of earning part of her college money, that Puff was a beef animal, not a family pet, didn't ease the pain. Only time would do that. Perhaps it was best that Jenny was leaving for camp in another week. A change of setting would help her forget. Seeing friends from last year, laughing and playing one last summer before she began the transformation from child into young woman was just what she needed right now.

Carole just wished Jenny could stay gone until Big Jim's barbecue was history, but she couldn't. School started in the third week of August, and Big Jim always served up the grand champion at his Labor Day event. Carole didn't usually go out of town for the long weekend, but this year, she would take her daughter somewhere far away from Ranger Springs. Someplace fun, with no animals to remind them of Puff's empty stall.

She'd nearly made it out of the barn when she saw a tall, broad-shouldered stranger standing in the wide doorway, staring at her in a way she didn't usually see in the light of day. Maybe in a smoky honky-tonk with a country-western tune playing in the jukebox...

She slowed, wondering if perhaps he was someone

she'd met a while back. Bright sunlight outlined his lean torso and long, straight legs. He'd dressed in jeans and a Western-cut plaid shirt, boots and a well-creased hat, but he didn't stand like a cowboy. The shade inside the barn, the deeper shadow beneath the brim of the Stetson, made him seem mysterious. Instead of tipping his hat or dropping his gaze, he continued to look his fill, even smiling just a bit like he knew some secret.

Carole tipped her chin up and broke eye contact. She didn't know this man. He wasn't from around here. And he was darn rude to boot.

"Congratulations on the win," he said as she walked by.

His deep, warm voice, totally without an accent, stopped her. "Thanks," she said, feeling more unsettled than ever now that she knew he'd been watching her—and Jenny—during the competition. "I don't know you, do I?"

"We haven't met yet," he said, turning toward her. The sun highlighted the right half of his face, showing smooth skin stretched over some mighty fine cheekbones. She suspected this man had his hair styled, not just cut like ordinary people, although she couldn't see much but a few short, dark-brown strands peeking from beneath his tan Stetson and around his well-shaped ears.

This was no weathered cowboy. From the way he was dressed, in new clothes and expensive boots, she'd be more likely to believe he was one of those models in *American Cowboy* magazine. He looked as good as one. As a matter of fact, he reminded her of her brother-in-law, Prince Alexi of Belegovia, when he'd dressed like Hank McCauley and fooled her sister

Kerry last summer. Alexi and Hank looked enough alike to be twins. Both were handsome as sin, but not as compelling as this stranger, in her opinion.

She realized she'd been giving the man a once-over for way too long. Not too many male-model types came to Ranger Springs, Texas, but that didn't excuse her ogling. Her mother would have called it downright rude.

"Greg Rafferty," he said with a smile, extending his hand. "And no, as I've already been reminded, I'm not from around here."

She laughed despite her suspicion over strangers and good-looking men who liked to undress women with their eyes. "I didn't mean to stare. The sun was in my eyes, and I couldn't tell if I'd seen you before."

She shook his hand, noticing his firm, enveloping grip that shot warmth all the way up her arm.

"I can't use the excuse of sun in my eyes. I'll admit I was staring."

He stated the offhand compliment with an intimate kind of amusement that made Carole blush.

She hadn't blushed in years. She thought she'd forgotten how. She'd apparently also forgotten how to shake hands, because she finally pulled away when she realized she'd been in his gentle grasp for about as long as she'd been staring at him moments ago.

"And you are…"

"I'm sorry. I'm still a little…excited about my daughter's win." She took a deep breath and looked into the blue-green eyes of the stranger. "Carole Jacks," she said, forcing herself to smile pleasantly when she wanted to gawk like a sixteen-year-old.

His expression changed from intimate interest to disbelief in a flash. Seconds later he blinked and schooled his features into a painfully benign mask. "You..." He swallowed, grimacing slightly. "I don't suppose you have another relative by the same name. A mother or aunt, perhaps?"

"I'm the only one around here that I know of," she said, more confused by the second.

"I was expecting someone a little...older." His eyes roamed over her body once more, and she felt that darn warmth seep through her, as hot at the Texas sun beating down on the metal roof above.

She shrugged off her hormone-induced condition. "Older?"

"I came to town expecting to find Alice, or maybe Aunt Bea, and instead I found—"

She stopped him before his eyes started wandering again. "What?"

"You know. Alice, that prototypical housekeeper on *The Brady Bunch*. And Aunt Bea was on—"

"*Andy Griffith*. Yes, I know, but what does that have to do with me? And why did you think I was older?"

"Because you bake cookies," he said, as though that would clear up everything.

"Cookies," she repeated carefully, wondering how someone this loony could be so good-looking.

"Yes. Ms. Carole's Cookies. Huntington Foods needs your help to—"

"Oh, no," she said, putting up both hands as if to ward him off. "I don't believe this." She took a step back, needing to put space between her and this...this city slicker. How could they have done this to her? Huntington had promised her no hassles, no demands. All they'd wanted were her cookie recipes. She'd written privacy clauses into her contract. She would never have licensed the rights to her cookies otherwise.

"Are you surprised that someone came down to see you?"

She nodded. "Darn right. Now you can just get back in your car or catch a plane back to Chicago."

"You don't know what I'm going to offer."

"My privacy is not for sale." She turned away, walking through the doorway and into the hot sunshine, leaving him standing in the shade of the barn.

Good thing she'd learned why he was here before she made an idiot of herself, acting like some silly teenager over a good-looking stranger. *Been there, done that.* Just because he had great bone structure and filled out his jeans didn't amount to a hill of beans. He could go straight to—

"Jenny," Carole whispered. Greg Rafferty might be low enough to try to get into her daughter's good graces. He could be on his way to her little girl right now, full of phony congratulations on her win, hoping to get to the mother through the daughter.

Halfway to the concession stand, Carole spun around, nearly colliding with the person behind her.

Strong hands steadied her. She looked up into Greg Rafferty's blue-green eyes. "You," she whispered. What was it about this man that sent her reeling—mentally and physically?

"You should get some signals installed if you're going to make turnarounds on a crowded thoroughfare," he said in a soft, deep voice that held more than a hint of amusement.

At her expense. "Let go." She brushed off his hold, then dusted her arms as though he'd left some trace.

Ridiculous. "Why were you following me?" she asked, deciding the best defense was a good offense.

"Because I came all the way from Chicago to see you, and you need to hear what I have to say."

She put her hands on her hips. "You're not going to give up, are you?"

"I can't." He shrugged. "I know about your contract, but things have changed. I need your cooperation."

Carole sighed. She was going to have to listen to him whether she wanted to or not. "Okay, you can buy me a soft drink and we'll sit in the shade. I'll give you ten minutes, then I need to get back to my daughter."

Within a few minutes they settled on a bench beneath a big cottonwood tree, just outside the barn. The familiar scents of sawdust, hay, animal sweat and manure grounded her in the present. By reminding her of the past, the attractive stranger sitting beside her filled her with insecurities over the future.

"So, why did you come all the way to Texas to talk me into something that is obviously opposite every privacy clause I had inserted into my contract with Huntington Foods?"

"I'm not sure if you heard about our previous C.E.O.'s very public argument with the 'food police,' but—"

"Yes, I heard about him calling the C.A.S.H.E.W. group a 'bunch of nuts.' Of course I was interested, since you produce my cookies. But like everything, the bad press he caused will pass."

He shook his head. "It's not that simple. When he, er, decided to resign, that also made news. And then the cable news outlets and primetime network shows started calling, asking for in-depth interviews. We're being compared to the tobacco industry executives who said, before Congress, 'I do not believe nicotine is addictive.' That kind of bad publicity doesn't go away until we clarify our position.''

Carole sat her soft drink on the bench with enough force that the liquid sloshed against the sides. "So clarify it. You're the new C.E.O., right? I don't see how—or why—my cooperation or endorsement would matter much."

"I'm not sure that you know this, but your cookies are our bestselling product. We'd like to design a publicity tour. Some select appearances on the afternoon talk shows and soft news segments, perhaps a demonstration of your baking techniques on the morning shows. And there's an upcoming food show we'd like for you to attend, perhaps as a featured presenter."

The idea of becoming a public figure filled her with so much dread that she had a hard time holding back a shudder. Her stomach clenched and her palms began to sweat, but she managed to hold herself together. *This was only his plan,* she told herself. *Not a reality.* Forcing a calmness she didn't feel, she managed to say flippantly, ''That's all, hmm?''

"Well, we'd need your permission to use your image on the packages. Oh, and we'd like to have some favorable articles written about you. Maybe with a photo spread of your home. You and your daughter sharing a plate of cookies. That sort of thing."

His plan grew worse and worse. She couldn't believe he would ask her to participate to this degree. She couldn't believe he'd expect her to put Jenny in…well, not danger, but potential emotional distress. But then, this new C.E.O. didn't know about her past.

Not very many people outside of her family and friends in Ranger Springs remembered.

"You have got to be kidding," she finally said.

"No." He appeared a little baffled. "We're not expecting anything unusual, Ms. Jacks."

She took a deep breath. "How about I just write you a nice letter. You can tell everyone that I agree— you're not really a rabidly crazy company who believes a high-sugar, high-fat diet is best for everyone."

He started to get a little red in the face. The heat? She didn't think so. She'd probably pushed him to the limit of his bottom-line heart.

"We'd like more than your vote of confidence, Ms. Jacks," he said in a very controlled voice. "And we're willing to pay quite a nice sum for your cooperation."

"Did you read my contract, Mr. Rafferty?"

"Greg, please. And, yes, I did."

"Then you know that I am under no obligation to publicize the cookies." The very idea caused another barely controlled shudder.

"Yes, I know, but as I've just explained, circumstances have changed."

"My position hasn't. Let me be perfectly clear. I don't want any publicity for myself or my family. My agreement with Huntington Foods has been perfect because my recipes are all that I had to give."

"Surely you could use the money."

"Not at the expense of my privacy," she stated, grabbing her soft drink and rising from the bench. "Now it's time for me to get back to my daughter. I hope you find another way to solve your problem, Greg Rafferty, because I am not going to change my mind."

She marched off toward the barn, but hadn't walked

more than four steps when she thought of one more point. "By the way, don't bother my daughter. She's off-limits, understand?"

"Why would you think I'd bother your daughter?" he asked, frowning at her.

"I know you big-business types. You're not above 'congratulating' her, too, just to get in my good graces. I'm telling you right now not to try it."

For some reason Greg Rafferty was like a burr under her saddle. The only way to relieve the irritation was to get rid of the irritant. She hoped he got the point and high-tailed it out of Texas.

"I would have congratulated her, if I'd seen her. But I saw you first. *Before* I knew who you were," he pointed out.

"So you say," she returned, knowing she couldn't trust his smooth-talking claims any farther than she could throw a twelve-hundred-pound steer. "Just leave, Mr. Rafferty. We're not buying what you're selling."

"I can be as stubborn as you are," he ground out.

"Maybe," she conceded, placing one hand on her hip. "But I own my land, and it's fenced in. If you cross my cattle guard, make sure you're ready for a fight, because I protect what's mine." She glared at him through narrowed eyes. "And I own a shotgun that I know how to use."

"Are you threatening me?" he asked incredulously.

"Just don't give me a reason to fill your backside with buckshot."

"I thought you Texans didn't shoot men in the back."

"We shoot varmints anywhere we please," she said, wishing she were back on her own property right now, safe behind the wire fencing and long driveway. Locked inside, where no one could bother her or her daughter.

He glared at her, but she'd seen and said enough. Carole spun on her heel, her boots digging into the dust-covered, dry grass. She felt his gaze burning into her back as surely as if he'd aimed his own weapon at her...at her backside.

He probably wasn't giving her the once-over now. He was scorching holes in her with angry eyes, she'd bet, although she'd die before she turned around to check.

She'd seen enough of Greg Rafferty. He'd better not show up on her property. Despite her bravado, she wouldn't really fill him with buckshot. No, she'd call Police Chief Parker and swear out a complaint. If Greg Rafferty didn't leave her alone, the only people baking Ms. Carole's cookies would be Ms. Carole herself.

Chapter Two

Greg planted both elbows on the darkened pine bar of Shultze's Roadhouse and mentally kicked himself for the hundredth time. Just because Carole Jacks possessed killer legs, a body to make a man drool, and sun-kissed hair he longed to run his fingers through, he should have behaved in a professional, rational manner. Hell, he'd practically drooled on her figure-molding white T-shirt and jeans. If he'd come on any stronger, she would have accused him of seducing her to get what he wanted.

Come to think of it, that would probably be better than the assumptions she'd come up with. Thinking he'd use her daughter to get to her.... What kind of low-life sleaze did she think he was? Using a kid...

He straightened, his hand closing around the frosty longneck as he remembered the look on the little girl's face as she'd realized she was going to lose that big steer to Big Jim's barbecue grill. Greg glanced at his watch. Nearly one o'clock. What time did that auction start? He thought he'd heard two, but after the confrontation with his sexy cowgirl, who'd turned out to be the woman he'd come all this way to see, he hadn't trusted his short-term memory. Hell, this whole trip to

Texas was turning into a journey to another dimension, not just a trip to a different state.

He had time to get back to the arena before the bidding started. If he did manage to buy the steer, Carole Jacks would automatically assume he'd done so to get into her good graces. She'd accuse him of trying to influence her daughter. He'd never be able to convince her he'd thought of outbidding Big Jim before he'd known who the country's favorite cookie queen was.

He should forget about the girl, the steer and the sexy cowgirl. Instead of planning to outbid the competition, he should put on his professional demeanor, just as he'd put on these cowboy clothes. Starting over again with Carole Jacks, beginning with an apology for his earlier outburst, was the only sensible strategy.

The plan not only sounded boring, but it totally ignored his feelings about saving the little girl's prize pet. He wasn't about to sit here sipping a cold one while some good ol' boy ripped the animal away from the child who'd raised him. Greg took a long drink of his beer, grinding his teeth as the vision took hold. He'd deal with Carole Jacks's suspicions after he handed the big black steer back to her daughter.

The fact that she'd be forced to deal with him at all was worth the expense of outbidding Big Jim. All he wanted was a fair chance to convince her that his plan was reasonable. Once she listened to him, calmly and without the overheated emotions of this afternoon, she might find she liked him. And if she softened just a bit, he'd have a chance to explore some of the nonprofessional aspects of their relationship.

Like the way her gaze had caressed him when they'd stood just inside the barn. The way she'd been interested in him as a man before she'd accused him of being a louse. He had a suspicion she'd rather eat dirt than admit she'd liked what she'd seen, but he knew a hungry look when he saw one. And Carole Jacks had an extraordinary pair of bedroom eyes that could arouse with just a glance. If he let his mind wander to what the rest of her could do, he'd never get to the auction in time.

With a last long swallow, Greg drained the long-neck and slid the empty bottle toward the inside edge of the bar. He retrieved his wallet from the back pocket of the stiff new jeans, then slapped a twenty on the ring-marked pine. That should cover his beer and a grilled cheese sandwich—in honor of Puff and steers everywhere. He just hoped he had enough cash in his debit account to afford a prize steer. If not, the arena had better take plastic, because he was going to buy that big black animal even if Carole Jacks assumed the worst.

This would all turn out well in the end. He *would* save Huntington Foods from the corporate equivalent of Big Jim's barbecue grill.

CAROLE WATCHED the bidders gather around the arena, spending more time talking to each other than looking at the animals inside the ring. And why not? They'd already decided which ones they'd bid on, and how much they were going to spend. The heifers they'd add to their breeding program, but the steers would all be used for some promotional or charitable event. Big Jim always bought the grand champion. He was gathering a crowd of cronies, his booming voice carrying across the ring.

Carole looked away from the overblown car dealer

to her daughter, who stood straight and silent beside Puff. She was so proud of Jenny, her little girl who was growing up fast. After dealing with not having a father all her life, she was now learning how to lose something she loved. Not that she hadn't known all along what Puff's fate would be. Staring the inevitable in the eye was far different from considering a nebulous circumstance, especially for a ten-year-old.

Carole realized with a jolt that her daughter was only seven years younger than she was when she'd met and run away with Johnny Ray French. He'd played guitar in a country-western band performing at the rodeo in San Antonio. She'd thought they'd fallen instantly in love. Probably more like lust, looking back. They'd taken off for his big chance to play The Grand Ol' Opry in Nashville, stopping in Arkansas to get married because, at heart, she was a good girl and that's how she'd been raised.

As though she was still seventeen, she clearly remembered how shocked she'd been when her nineteen-year-old husband, drunk on beer and a taste of fame, practically made love to another woman in front of the cameras filming a documentary about the band. And that was right after she'd discovered she was pregnant. Talk about life throwing you a curve! She'd been afraid to call home, embarrassed to admit her stupidity to her mother and two sisters.

Fortunately, her mother saw the documentary on television and left immediately in the family sedan to bring her middle daughter home.

Back in Ranger Springs, Carole had wanted to pretend that nothing was wrong, that she hadn't run away with a huge jerk and wasn't going to blow up like a balloon in just a few months. But she had. Her tooled leather belt with the engraved silver buckle had gone only halfway around her middle. She'd waddled where she'd once strutted her stuff in tight jeans and body-hugging, snap-front shirts. She'd held her head up and pretended not to notice the stares of her neighbors, her classmates and her former teachers. Her family had stood beside her, saddened but determined to see her through her impetuous "mistake." Her mother had gotten her out of her teenage marriage…and Johnny Ray had never wanted to see his child.

Carole leaned her chin on her crossed arms, resting on top of the wooden rail, and sighed. Up until the moment Jenny had been born, she hadn't decided whether she was going to keep her child or give her up for adoption. She used to place her hands on her big belly and wonder what would be best for her baby—a single mother with only a high school education, or a two-parent household with educated people who desperately wanted a child.

Once she'd held the baby in her arms, the decision was made; she loved Jenny on sight. She'd vowed right then to be the best mother possible, to give her baby love and attention, and provide an extended family including a grandmother, aunts and lots of friends. And Jenny had grown into an intelligent, sensitive, talented daughter. In her totally unbiased opinion, of course.

And now her daughter was getting a lesson in life that had to be learned at some point. That didn't make it any easier to watch.

"All you bidders gather 'round," the announcer called out from the box overlooking the stalls and chutes. "We'll start our bidding for our grand champion, owned and shown by Miss Jennifer Jacks, at one thousand dollars.''

Carole watched her daughter bravely lead Puff to the center of the ring. Jenny had cried all her tears; she'd said her goodbyes and was ready to accept a check to go into her college fund. The outcome was certain, but they all had to go through the formality of watching and listening to Big Jim bellow out his bids. Across the arena, Carole heard his friends cheer him on, motivated, no doubt, by the thought of a choice serving of barbecue come Labor Day.

"Fifteen hundred from Ralph Biggerstaff," the announcer stated.

Big Jim bellowed out, "Two thousand."

Well, at least Jenny would be able to choose her college with a bit more freedom. And she wouldn't have to work part-time unless she wanted to. That was good.

"Twenty-one hundred," a different voice called out. A deep voice, without inflection or accent.

No! He wouldn't! With an angry frown, Carole stepped up onto the bottom rail and searched the opposite side of the ring for the source of her irritation.

There he stood, tan Stetson covering the upper part of his face with shadow. She recognized his shirt, though, and those brand-new jeans. Was he bidding just to irritate her, or was he seriously considering buying Puff? If he thought he'd impress her by paying more than Big Jim, he had another think coming. She ought to march right over there and tell him she wasn't about to accept his money. Or Huntington's money. Had they authorized something this low, or was Greg Rafferty a runaway wagon?

"Twenty-two hundred," Big Jim announced confidently.

"Twenty-three," Rafferty said in an amused tone.

So, he thought this was funny, did he? Carole jumped down from the fence. She'd go over there and tell him again what he obviously didn't believe this afternoon; she didn't want to listen to his big plans for Ms. Carole's Cookies, and she didn't want him using her daughter.

"Twenty-four hundred," Big Jim said, irritation obvious in his booming voice as Carole marched around the ring.

"Twenty-five."

Show-off, Carole wanted to yell. Her boots couldn't navigate through the deep dirt of the arena fast enough. When she got her hands on him…

"Twenty-six hundred," Big Jim ground out, his voice showing more than irritation now. He sounded downright mean.

Greg Rafferty hadn't seen mean yet. When she got her hands on him—

"Three thousand," he said.

An audible gasp filled the big metal barn, followed by whispered comments. Carole stumbled, finding the metal rail with one shaking hand. For the first time she realized how odd this must appear to the rest of the folks witnessing the bidding. A stranger, a man they've never seen before, challenging Big Jim for the grand champion.

She held on to the rail and looked to the center of the ring, guiltily thinking about Jenny for the first time since Greg Rafferty started bidding. Her daughter appeared confused by the war going on between the two men. She'd expected Big Jim to buy Puff. She didn't know this other man. She certainly hadn't heard that he'd come to Texas to sweet-talk her mother into doing something unthinkable to save Huntington's reputation.

What about my own reputation? she wanted to shout. True, Greg Rafferty didn't know about her past. He didn't accept how averse to publicity she was. But darn it, for ten years—with the exception of the foreign paparazzi who'd come to town back when Kerry Lynn was with Prince Alexi—everyone had forgotten her teenage behavior. They'd let her keep her emotional baggage stored very neatly in the back of the closet, where it didn't bother anyone.

"This has got to stop," Carole muttered, pushing away from the rail and marching toward the man who was giving her a pounding headache, not to mention causing her heart to ache for the little girl caught in the middle.

"Three thousand once."

Carole zeroed in on him, maybe twenty feet away. He turned to watch her approach, what she had to assume was a gloating expression on his model-handsome face.

"Three thousand twice."

She abandoned her plan to punch him in the nose. Besides going against her generally antiviolent approach to life, he'd probably have her arrested for assault. Instead, she grabbed two fistsful of his shirt as soon as she got within snatching distance of him.

"Sold for three thousand dollars to the stranger in the blue-plaid shirt."

She stumbled as she tried to shake some sense into him, even though it was too late. Even though he'd already outbid Big Jim for the right to turn Puff into sirloin and hamburger.

He steadied her with two large hands to her waist. "Be careful," he said, his tone amused as he looked down at her. "You don't have to be so enthusiastic with your appreciation."

"Go to hell," she said through clenched teeth.

Thelma Rogers rushed up, eyes aglow, camera dangling. "What an exciting auction! I need a photo for the *Gazette*."

"No!" Carole nearly shouted. Inside she was shaking, angry and protective and yes, afraid. Afraid of him dragging her into his publicity campaign without her permission. Afraid he was digging around in her closet for all her emotional baggage. No one had that right. Just because she'd sold them some cookie recipes—

"Why not?" Rafferty asked.

"I don't do photos," she snapped at him. "If you want one with your new steer, you go right ahead. Just keep me out of it." She paused and narrowed her eyes. "And keep Jenny out of it, too."

"That's okay," Thelma said tentatively, looking between the two of them. "I already took one of Jenny with the steer when she won the championship earlier."

"Great. Then that should be fine for the paper."

"Yes, I don't think we need a photo of Ms. Jacks assaulting me."

Thelma glanced between them, then said, "I think I'll go over and see what's happening with the heifers."

Good idea, Carole thought. "I did not assault you," she ground out as, from of the corner of her eye, she saw a crowd gathering. The last thing she wanted was an audience for what she had to say to this annoying man, so she turned her back on her neighbors, hoping they'd take the hint. "I just want you to go away and leave us alone."

"I already told you why I came down here. If you'd just keep an open mind, we might make some progress."

"Progress! I suppose you think you know what's best for me and my family?"

Greg Rafferty put his hands on his hips and looked around. Her friends and neighbors looked back, although at least they were keeping their distance. Slowly he smiled as he turned back to her. "For someone who thinks she knows just what she wants, you seem to have a little problem executing your plans."

"Not until you showed up," she said, pointing her finger at him. She couldn't stand a smug man, and this one had smugness down to a science. He knew he was darned good-looking, even in clothes he obviously didn't wear every day. The fact that he could carry off wearing the "uniform" of a cowboy instead of what had to be more familiar—the uniform of a businessman—said a lot about how much confidence he had. Not that she admired his guts. Not at all.

"All I wanted to do was talk to you."

"Then why did you buy Puff?"

"Puff?" He looked toward the ring, his smile returning. "That big black beast's name is Puff?" he asked with nearly contagious amusement.

"Jennifer named him," Carole admitted, turning to watch her daughter walk toward them. "And don't upset her any more than she already is. She got too attached to him. I knew this was going to be a problem, but I couldn't stop her from loving that stupid steer.''

''I have no intention of upsetting her. In fact, that's why I bid on him.''

''What are you talking about?'' Carole asked, turning back to search his face for the truth.

''Before I knew who you were, I noticed how sensitive she was. When the guy standing nearby told me what happened to the grand champion steer, I decided to buy him myself.''

''What…what are you going to do with a steer?''

Before he could answer, Jenny stopped at the fence, Puff in tow.

''Mom, what are you doing over here?'' she asked in an accusing tone that only a child could achieve. ''Everyone's looking!''

Carole moaned inside. She wanted to sink into the soft dirt and pretend this day had never existed. ''I'm just talking to Mr. Rafferty, honey. That's all.''

''Mom, you grabbed him!''

Carole narrowed her eyes and frowned at the object of her frustration. ''Just his shirt.''

He smiled back. She wanted to shake him, then swing him around and put a boot to his backside. So much for her nonviolent tendencies. The faster he got out of town, the quicker life could return to normal. She and Jenny would go back to their nice, calm life.

Dismissing her glare, he turned to Jenny. ''Hi. My name is Greg Rafferty, and I think your steer is…well, he's a good-looking animal.''

''Yeah, he is, and he's nice, too.'' Her young face fell. ''But I guess that doesn't matter anymore.''

''What do you mean?''

Carole acknowledged that he sounded genuinely

confused, which was an act, of course. He'd known what he was doing all along—searching her out, buying the steer, making her pay attention to him when all she wanted was to be left alone.

"Since you bought him, I guess you're going to have a…a barbecue like Big Jim."

Carole heard the quaver in her daughter's voice, saw the way her lip trembled when she stumbled over the word that signified the fate of all the grand champion steers. She wanted to reach across the metal railing and hug Jenny close, but her daughter wouldn't appreciate the public display any more than Carole appreciated public attention of any kind.

"No, no, I'm not," Rafferty said in a gentle voice that surprised Carole as much as his claim. "I don't want to take your steer away from you."

"But you bought him," Jenny said.

"Only because I needed to outbid Big Jim," he said with a wink. "I couldn't let that big airbag buy a steer as nice as Puff."

Jenny giggled.

Carole blinked, not sure she'd heard him correctly. This was the businessman who wanted to violate her contract? This man who spoke so gently to her daughter, and made her laugh? And what did he mean that he didn't want to take Puff away from Jenny?

"Wait a minute," Carole said. "What are you going to do with him if you aren't planning some…event like Big Jim's?"

He smiled broadly, looking between her and her daughter. Just like the cowboy he was pretending to be, he puffed up a little bigger as he spoke to Jenny. "I saw how attached you were to your steer. I've never had anything that large myself, but I did have a dog when I was about your age. I thought maybe you'd like to keep Puff.''

"Keep him?'' Jenny asked, looking really confused as her hand tightened around Puff's lead rope.

"Sure. I know I bought him, but I'm going to sign him back over to you and your mom. That way, you won't ever have to worry about Big Jim getting his hooks on Puff again.''

"Wait just a minute,'' Carole interrupted, holding up her hand for silence. "You can't just give Puff back to Jenny. Besides, I don't trust your motives.''

"I already told you—''

"And I told you I don't trust you.''

"But, Mom—''

"Not now, Jenny.'' Carole put her hands on her hips and faced Greg Rafferty. "You bought that steer fair and square at the auction, Mr. Greg Rafferty. You can't give him back.''

"Of course I can. I know some people might think it's extravagant, but—''

"That's not what I'm thinking at all,'' she said, narrowing her eyes at him. "And I don't mean that you *shouldn't* give him back. I mean you *can't* give him back.''

"Mom—''

"Now, Jenny, I know this is hard for you, but we all have to accept the fact that Mr. Rafferty owes three thousand dollars toward your college fund, and he now owns Puff.''

"I don't want to own Puff!''

"Mr. Rafferty,'' Carole said, leaning close and saying each word succinctly, "that steer eats about thirty-five pounds of feed each day. Even though I've grown a little attached to him, too, I don't want to own him, either.''

GREG USED his monogrammed handkerchief to wipe the sweat and dirt from his forehead, wincing at the sight of dark, wet smears across the white linen. So this is why cowboys wear bandannas, he thought as he leaned against the fence and watched his three thousand-dollar rack of prime rib graze contentedly in the rented pasture.

''This is all your fault,'' he muttered to the unconcerned steer, even though he knew the culprit didn't have four legs. No, Greg acknowledged, at least to himself, yesterday he'd gotten himself into this mess by making a bunch of assumptions. The words of a college professor came back to haunt him: ''*Assume* makes an *ass* out of *u* and *me.*'' Well, he'd made one big fool of himself this afternoon. Every action he'd taken had dug him deeper and deeper into a pit of mistakes and culture clashes.

Of course, Carole Jacks hadn't helped him dig his way out of the hole. In fact, she seemed happy to shovel dirt in around him as he'd flailed away, wondering which way was up. The only thing he'd been sure of was that he was even more attracted to Carole Jacks, reclusive cookie queen, than he was to his blond cowgirl.

Damned if he could figure out why, though. She fought him at every opportunity. She made a point of showing how much she disliked him, making a scene yesterday at the arena even though she claimed she hated publicity. Maybe she felt comfortable enough around her neighbors to be a bit more...expressive.

So maybe the attraction he felt for her wasn't one-sided. Maybe she felt it, too, and that frightened her. He had no doubt she really didn't believe him, or trust his motives. That obstacle didn't bother him, because she was obviously the kind of person who needed proof. Simply telling her that he hadn't bought Puff, the grand champion steer, to impress her didn't carry much weight with Carole Jacks.

A smile spread across Greg's face as he recalled the way she'd grabbed his shirt. And the way his hands had settled so naturally around her waist, as though they belonged there and nowhere else.

At least, nowhere he could put them in public.

Thinking about Carole Jacks made him even hotter than this Texas summer. Not even noon and the temperature must be nearly ninety degrees! Pushing away from the wooden fence post, Greg walked through the brown, dying grass toward the brick and frame house he'd rented late yesterday afternoon. As soon as he'd realized he was stuck with Puff—at least temporarily—he'd looked up realty companies in the phone book and made an appointment with a cute, efficient redheaded lady named Gina Summers.

Fortunately, this house had been available on a monthly lease. Fully furnished, it was more than he needed, but at least he'd be comfortable during his stay in Ranger Springs, Texas. He walked up the three steps to the front porch, pulled open the storm door and slipped into the absolute necessity of air-conditioning.

Of course, if Carole Jacks hadn't been so bull-headed, he thought as he walked across the hardwood floors toward the back patio, she could have taken the steer home with her. Greg would have been more than happy to check into a hotel or motel until he could convince her to modify her contract with Huntington Foods. Everyone, including Jenny and Puff, would have been much more content with that arrangement. But leasing a house and forty acres for a month was just another example of how unusual this trip had become.

At least the house had a pool. He loved to swim, and having the water to himself rather than sharing it with fifteen screaming kids at a hotel was worth a lot. He didn't particularly enjoy children, maybe because he hadn't been around them very much. His older brother, Brad, the hotheaded former C.E.O. of his mother's family-owned company, hadn't married yet. Neither had his younger sister, Stephanie, the current C.F.O. of Huntington Foods. Some of his college friends were married, but most of them had babies, and they got baby-sitters when he went out with them.

Older children like Jennifer were okay, he guessed, but he struggled to talk to them intelligently. At least with her he'd had a topic of conversation. One of his biggest fears was being left alone with a small child who wanted to talk. He was afraid he'd say the wrong thing.

Just like everything else he'd done or thought since arriving at the county livestock arena, his attention came back to Carole Jacks. His blond cowgirl. The object of his professional quest. The mother of a ten-year-old girl with a pet who ate thirty-five pounds of feed a day. Plus grass and hay, he'd been informed by a helpful rancher at the arena.

With a sigh, cursing his luck for becoming mentally obsessed and physically attracted to a woman who was all wrong for him, Greg began removing his clothes, all the way down to the stretchy black Speedo beneath those stiff new jeans.

He'd take a swim right now. The exercise would do him good, and maybe the water would be cold enough to take his mind—and other parts of his body—off the exciting, unusual Ms. Carole.

Chapter Three

"I can't believe you talked me into this," Carole said as she drove up the gravel road toward the formerly empty brick house. Only Jenny's overly dramatic reminder that she'd be leaving for camp soon and might not ever see Puff again had prodded Carole into finding out where Rafferty had holed up.

"Why don't you like him, Mom?" Jenny asked, leaning forward to see over the dash of Carole's pickup. "I thought he was pretty nice."

Carole sighed, remembering the way her normally reserved daughter had actually giggled—giggled, for heaven's sake!—at Greg Rafferty's teasing comments yesterday. He had charmed her daughter, but his obvious talents weren't going to work on the mother. No way. All she had to do was keep reminding herself that he was a businessman whose only concern was his company. He didn't even care that she had a very clear, very valid contract with Huntington Foods! Before he'd come to Ranger Springs, she'd been perfectly happy with her arrangement, which allowed her the financial freedom to work part-time baking desserts for the Four Square Café and giving cooking classes at upscale retail stores periodically in Austin and San Antonio. Most of all, she got to be a full-time mother to Jenny.

But she did owe her daughter an explanation of why Greg Rafferty wasn't the greatest thing since sliced bread, just because he'd saved Puff from Big Jim's big Labor Day chow-down.

"He's in Texas to convince me to change my agreement with Huntington Foods, Jenny. Even after I told him I wasn't interested in his proposal, he came back to the arena and bid on your steer. His motives seem pretty obvious to me."

"What do you mean?"

Carole winced as the pickup hit a pothole in the gravel road. She steered to the other side of the drive and slowed down. "I mean he bought Puff because he thought it would get him in our good graces."

"Mom, he spent *three thousand dollars!* Are you sure he's just trying to get you to change your agreement? And what kind of things does he want you to do?"

"He wants me to do all kinds of things! Go on a publicity tour, make television appearances and get interviewed by everyone and their cousin. He wants my picture on the cookie packages, and worst of all, he wants people to write articles about *us.* He tried to make it sound very normal, like I should be glad to do this for him." She snorted in a very unladylike way that she hoped Jenny didn't emulate. "I'm not about to change my life just to help his company get out of some bad publicity."

"That's kind of stubborn of you," Jenny observed with the wisdom of youth. "If I said something like that, you'd get after me for being bullheaded."

Carole smiled. "You're probably right, honey, but

believe me, I don't want to become a public figure. Once you do, there's no end to the things people can say about you.''

"So did you explain all that to him?"

"Oh, I think he knows exactly how I feel."

Carole pulled behind a luxury auto parked on the concrete pad in front of the garage. A discreet sticker on the bumper identified the rental car company. Greg Rafferty obviously went first-class, from his extravagant gestures of "goodwill" to his expensive new boots. And he was the kind of man who could pull off such shows of wealth, with his lean but muscular build and model good looks.

He probably spent a lot of time posturing in front of a full-length mirror, she speculated as she turned the key to kill the engine. He'd better not object to her parking their four-year-old, slightly battered pickup in the same driveway as his fancy rental car, because she wouldn't mind giving him another piece of her mind.

"Mom, you're getting that look on your face again."

Carole nearly jumped at the sound of Jenny's voice. She'd blocked out everything but the infuriating man who'd come to town just to torment her. For the second time in as many days, he'd made her forget her daughter. Another black mark against Greg Rafferty.

"Sorry, honey. I was just thinking about what I was going to say to Mr. Rafferty when I saw him."

"You're not going to yell at him again, are you?"

"I never yell." She didn't meet her daughter's eyes, scanning the darkened windows of the house for signs of movement.

"Yes, you do, and you look really mad." Jenny

placed her hand on Carole's arm, bringing her attention back to the interior of the pickup. "You should think about what he wants you to do. Maybe you could do just a little bit. He seemed like a nice man."

"Jenny, just because he was nice to you doesn't mean his intentions are good."

"But you always tell me to keep an open mind when I meet new people. I'm just saying you should do the same thing."

Carole reached for the door handle. "Okay, I'll talk to him again. But I'm not promising to agree with him. I like our life just fine, thank-you-very-much."

Jenny giggled at their familiar banter. From the beginning, they'd been closer than mother and daughter. Without a father around to distract them, they'd clung to each other through good times and bad. Carole had once worried that Jenny would suffer from not having a dad, but with the help of friends and relatives, they'd coped just fine. Jenny rarely talked about her biological father anymore, and for that, Carole was grateful. Her ex hadn't wanted a child ten years ago; he didn't deserve one now.

"I don't see Puff," Jenny said as Carole rang the door bell.

"He's probably in the shade of those cottonwood trees by the stock tank, or maybe inside the barn."

"I hope Mr. Rafferty knows how to take care of him. Puff isn't used to being outside all day. His coat will just fry in this sun."

Carole smiled, glad that her daughter was thinking about her former steer's welfare rather than his imminent trip to the meat packer's. "You can tell Mr. Rafferty what he needs to know. I doubt he knows anything about cattle other than what he learned yesterday at the arena.''

There was no answer to her summons, so she rang the bell again, folded her hands across her chest and tried not to concentrate on all of his faults, much less wishing him a miserable stay in Texas. Thinking such thoughts wasn't exactly the charitable thing to do for a Sunday visit.

''Maybe he's outside with Puff,'' Jenny speculated.

''Okay. Let's walk around back and see.''

The drone of the air-conditioning unit kept Carole from hearing anything that would give away Rafferty's location. They walked toward the small barn that had been vacant a long time. The former owners hadn't run any cattle or horses on their small ranch since their kids had outgrown 4-H.

''Puff!'' Jenny called out, looking over the fence to the dark interior of the barn.

A dusky shadow moved, then slowly materialized into the large shape of Jenny's steer—or her former steer, Carole corrected herself. She held her breath, wondering if Rafferty was also in the barn, until she realized what she was doing. She resisted the urge to call out to the man, to find out where he was lurking. With a disgusted sigh, she looked around the pasture, finding no trace of him.

''Do you want to stay and see Puff? I'm going back to the house to find Mr. Rafferty.''

''I'll stay in the barn, Mom.'' Jenny unlatched the gate and hurried toward the steer.

''Don't wander off,'' Carole warned as she walked toward the house.

The sun beat down on her back and shoulders, reminding her that she hadn't worn a hat. And why was that? Because she wanted to look less like a cowgirl and more like a woman. A twenty-eight-year-old mother, a single head of her household, who had no business worrying about how she looked to visit a man who no doubt wanted her to dress up in an old-fashioned ruffled apron, display a plate of cookies and smile for the cameras.

But a little bit of doubt remained about her motives. Far back in her mind, she wondered if she'd dressed in soft, worn, body-hugging jeans and fitted, Western-cut shirt to make Greg Rafferty's gaze roam over her the way he'd done yesterday at the arena. Could she possibly enjoy enticing his interest when she didn't like him as a person? Surely she wasn't that shallow.

She nearly stumbled over an exposed rock when she realized that she *was* exactly that superficial. With no conscious awareness, she was soliciting the interest of a man who was here to coax her into doing something she didn't want to do, who would go to endless trouble and expense to impress her from a professional stand-point. Why, he was probably acting interested in her as another coercion tactic!

By the time she arrived back at the house, she was flushed from more than the heat. Something about Greg Rafferty rubbed her the wrong way. She'd never had this reaction to another man. In the past ten years, not once had she been even slightly tempted by the wrong kind of guy. Eleven years ago, as flighty as a green-broke filly...now that was a different story.

Carole pushed open the gate on the side of the house, grateful for the slight shade under the roof overhang. As soon as she turned the corner into the backyard, however, she was back in the sunlight again. She blinked, then squinted, then stared. Standing beside the pool, dressed in what could only be described as a scrap of black fabric stretched across an incredible male butt, stood the best-looking man her imagination could have dreamed up.

He must have heard her enter the yard because he turned, giving her a different view. His backside wasn't the only part of his anatomy that scrap of a swimsuit struggled to cover. She sucked in a deep breath through her mouth, then started coughing.

Rafferty advanced on her until she put up a hand to stop him. If he got too close, she wasn't real sure what she'd do. His lean, muscular body glistened with drops of water that slid from his wide shoulders to his smooth chest, then down his stomach, racing toward the low band of black fabric. She had the insane urge to taste those drops of water before they made their final destination.

After all, she was awfully thirsty.

She closed her eyes, thankful that she'd stopped coughing, hoping she could control these wild, out-of-character urges that had suddenly taken over her psyche. She wasn't a loose woman. She wasn't desperate. But she had been celibate for most of her adult life. Maybe there was something to those articles about hormones kicking in when a woman approached thirty.

"Are you all right?"

Without opening her eyes, she could tell he was close. Too close. Water-drop-licking close. "I'm fine," she managed to whisper. Directing her gaze about six feet off the ground, she opened her eyes.

"I thought I was going to have to pound you on the back," he said in an amused tone. "Or maybe give you the Heimlich maneuver."

"I'll take my chances on choking."

Rafferty laughed. "You still don't trust me."

I don't trust myself, she wanted to say, but kept silent. She found the idea of him locking his arms around her from behind, pressing that damp, hard body against her as his hands put pressure right below her breasts, way too tempting.

"You surprised me," she said, trying to explain why she'd gone loco at the sight of him. "I rang the bell earlier, but no one answered."

"I like to swim."

Which meant he spent lots of time in such abbreviated attire. Or, if he had his own pool, maybe none at all. "Really?" Carole swallowed again, this time more successfully.

"Mmm-hmm," he said, his gaze taking in her shirt and jeans. She felt extremely overdressed, considering his state, but then reminded herself that she certainly didn't need to be wearing any less around Greg Rafferty. *He's all wrong for you,* she warned herself, even as she stopped her wayward eyes and thoughts from drifting southward.

"I'm glad you came to see me, but I am rather surprised. You weren't thrilled that I bought your daughter's steer."

"My daughter? Yes, my daughter! She's in the barn. That's why we came to see you. Both of us. Because she wanted to make sure you knew how to take care of Puff."

"Both of you," he repeated, sounding disappointed. He ran a hand through his thick, wet hair.

"Yes. As a matter of fact, I'd better go check on her." She tore her gaze away from his face and turned around, ready to hurry back to the barn. Ready to drive her pickup down that gravel road as if the devil himself was chasing her.

The devil in a black Speedo.

His hand stopped her, clamped around her upper arm gently but firmly. She felt the dampness through her suddenly thin cotton shirt and shivered. "Wait a minute. Let me get a towel and I'll go with you."

So much for making a hasty retreat. "You need more than a towel," she said before thinking.

He let go of her arm, then shrugged when she looked at him. "I wasn't expecting company."

"Apparently not," Carole murmured, cursing herself for giving him another once-over with her wickedly independent eyes. Why couldn't her body obey her firm resolve not to pay the least amount of attention to this totally unsuitable man?

"Are you shocked by what I'm wearing, Ms. Carole?" Rafferty asked in a teasing tone.

"You don't have anything I haven't seen before," she replied, folding her arms across her chest and looking over the high fence toward the barn. Not that she could see anything.

She wasn't about to tell him that she hadn't seen anything exactly like he displayed. If the rest of him was as good as— *Don't go there,* she warned herself. *Stop thinking about him that way!*

"I'll bet you don't have a lot of cowboys running around in competitive swimwear," he said with a chuckle. "I assume the community is a little more conservative than that."

"You've got that right," Carole agreed, still not looking at him. "We tend to be a bit more modest."

"So you think I'm an exhibitionist for swimming in my own pool?"

"I didn't call you names."

"You didn't have to," he said, his voice coming from very close beside her. She couldn't resist looking.

"Is this better?" He held his arms out, revealing a partially buttoned cotton shirt and a yellow towel wrapped around his waist.

"Different," she admitted with a smile. He didn't look sophisticated and urban at the moment. Tousled and with the strange get-up, no one could consider him a threat to anyone's peace of mind.

Of course, she still remembered what he looked like without the shirt and towel.

"I do have some questions that you and Jenny can answer," he said as they started walked toward the gate, "about feeding Puff. What time, how much at a time, that sort of thing."

He was right behind her, and Carole could swear that she felt his hot breath on her neck. Ridiculous. Her mind was playing tricks on her. The weather was warm, the pool made the breeze humid.

"What's that perfume you're wearing?" he asked as he reached around her to open the gate.

"I'm not wearing any," she managed to answer as she squeezed through the opening.

"Really? You smell like vanilla."

"I baked this morning," she admitted, walking quickly toward the barn.

"A batch of Ms. Carole's cookies?" he asked in an amused tone.

She turned back and frowned at him. "No, coffee cake. There's more to life than cookies, Mr. Rafferty."

His gaze roamed over her jeans and shirt, pausing to look her in the eye. "I'm aware of that, Ms. Jacks."

She set her lips in a thin line and turned back to where her daughter was waiting. Irritating man. She should have said, "There's more to life than cookies *and sex.*"

CAROLE WAVED as Jenny scrambled into the back seat of the minivan with her friends Ashley and Meagan. The other two moms had offered to take the three girls to San Antonio for a day at their favorite amusement park, Schlitterbahn. Which was great for Jenny, because it took her mind off the auction and distracted her from the present location of Puff. Carole was pretty sure she'd want to go over there twice a day if possible.

Jenny had giggled yesterday at Greg Rafferty's towel-wrapped ensemble, but Carole hadn't laughed. Not when she remembered how he'd looked *before* he'd covered up. There was only so much potent male she could tolerate before retreating to the safety of her home. And staying there.

Except today he was invading her space, courtesy of the invitation she'd grudgingly extended. Jenny had insisted on open-mindedness, and Carole wouldn't disappoint her daughter. That didn't mean she would agree to whatever Rafferty was suggesting.

As soon as the minivan was out of sight, Carole sighed and walked into the house. The absolute silence reminded her that in another week, Jenny would be gone to camp and every day would sound like this. Quiet. Still. After growing up in a small house with two sisters, then having a baby of her own, she wasn't accustomed to what some people called peaceful. She much preferred the sound of her daughter's chatter, the ding-ding of electronic games, the singsong nature of children's music.

Even Puff was gone, living at the rented house with a man from Chicago who didn't know alfalfa pellets from sweet feed.

And said stranger was going to arrive here in less than an hour.

With a sigh, she switched on the radio and let the sound of soft rock—since she no longer listened to country music—fill the silent kitchen as she gazed outside. A side bay window overlooked the pasture, but there wasn't much there to see today. The Texas sun had bleached the grass to a pale golden beige, and until the rains came again in September, the fields would remain lifeless.

"Why did I agree to meet with him?" Carole mumbled as she smelled the coffee still simmering in the bottom of the glass carafe. She wrinkled her nose at the foul odor, quickly pouring out the dark liquid. She wasn't mean enough to serve that gunk to Rafferty, even if they were adversaries.

Of course, she thought with a smile, she might be able to convince him that "real cowboys" drank that kind of hot acid, but she wasn't about to subject her stomach to such abuse. She'd make a fresh pot right before he arrived, but darned if she was going to bake any cookies to go along with the coffee. No way. This was strictly business.

GREG PULLED TO A STOP in the gravel driveway behind the nondescript white pickup truck that Carole had driven to his rental property yesterday. Perhaps today they could focus on the issue to Huntington Foods' image problem—if they could ignore the sexual attraction that simmered right below the surface of her incredibly smooth, vanilla-scented skin.

He promised himself he'd try as he exited the air-conditioned interior of his rental car for the sauna heat of Texas in August. How did these people stand it? At least he had the pool to help him cool off. He enjoyed the luxury of swimming anytime he wanted, although he felt a bit guilty about not working harder on getting this situation straightened out. He hadn't become C.E.O. of his family's business by lying around a pool—much less daydreaming about Carole Jacks.

And he wouldn't solve Huntington's problem by lusting after their "cash cow," which was a terrible misnomer, he thought with a frown as he rang the doorbell to her modest brick home. He could either deal with her on a professional level or appeal to her on a private one. He couldn't do both.

She'd added some homey touches to her house, he noticed as he waited for her to answer the doorbell. A wreath of twisted vines and sunflowers adorned the dark-red front door. A window box of multicolored flowers around the side of the house added color to the brown-speckled brick and beige trim. Even in the flower beds beside the walkway, painted rocks and a few seashells made them special. He assumed Jenny had some hand in those decorations. Overall, the Jacks residence looked very nice and inviting.

"Hello," she said a bit breathlessly as she opened the dark-red panel all the way, then flicked open the storm door. She smoothed her hair back from her cheek in an unconscious gesture, leaving a slight smudge of flour as she took a deep breath. Three of the buttons on her Western-style shirt threatened to pop.

Oh, man, was he in trouble. Personally, professionally, every which way he could manage.

His gaze jerked from her breasts to her face. "I hope I didn't interrupt something," Greg said, taking the open door as a summons to enter. He hadn't worn his new Stetson today, but he imagined quite a few cowboys had come calling through this doorway, removing their hats as they waited for Carole Jacks to smile at them.

"No," she said, taking a step back and wiping her hands on her jeans-covered thighs, "I was just doing something in the kitchen."

He had a mental flash of hooking his hands around her thighs, lifting her to the kitchen counter and exploring every inch of her vanilla-scented body.

Not a good beginning to a business meeting, he told himself as she gestured toward the couch and chairs in the living room. *Oh, yes. Those would work, too.*

"Where's Jenny?" he asked, looking around the country-style furnishings that featured little-girl touches and several framed ribbons. He needed a buffer, something to take his mind off Carole Jacks, the desirable woman.

"Gone with friends to San Antonio for the day." She paused. "Thank you for listening to her advice yesterday and inviting her to visit Puff. She's still experiencing some separation anxiety."

"So's the steer. Last night he bawled like a baby."

"I'm sorry," Carole said with amusement in her voice. "Jenny is apparently doing better than Puff."

"Don't worry about it. He was fine after I gave him an extra scoop of feed." Greg grinned. "Of course, I could bring him back here anytime. I'd even contribute a substantial amount to his feed bill.''

Carole rolled her eyes and ignored his comment. ''Take a seat. Would you like some coffee? I just made a pot.''

''Coffee would be great. Black is fine.''

She took a deep breath, which again threatened the buttons on her blue plaid shirt. ''I'll be right back.''

Greg wandered into the small living room and put his portfolio down on the couch. He saw evidence of Carole's homey touch in the fresh-cut flowers on the pine table and the stenciling around the top of the wall.

Within moments she was back with a tray, mugs, and a coffeepot. ''Make yourself comfortable, Mr. Rafferty.''

''Please, call me Greg,'' he reminded her again.

They settled on opposite ends of the sofa, and she handed him a mug of coffee. ''Would you like a cookie?''

He couldn't hold back a grin at the irony. ''Sure.'' He took a bite and let the taste roll around on his tongue like a fine wine. ''A new recipe?'' he finally asked when he couldn't identify the specific product.

She nodded.

''These definitely aren't Prairie Pralines, or Chisolm Trail Chocolate Chip, or even Stampede Surprise.''

She raised her eyebrow at his recitation of her recipes, smiling slightly. ''These don't have a name yet, but what do you think?''

''I think Huntington would love to get the recipe,'' he answered, reaching for another one. ''I'm no expert on food, but I'm tasting pecans, vanilla and chocolate chunks. What's that other ingredient?''

"A secret," she said, sitting back against the couch. "I didn't fix them to entice you with a new recipe."

"Ms. Carole," he said in his best imitation of a Western drawl, "darn near everything about you is enticing."

She looked shocked, then she laughed. He hadn't seen her so amused before, and the joy transformed her face from beautiful to radiant. Her eyes crinkled and her cheeks took on a darker shade of pink. He wanted to hold on to the warmth that flowed so freely from this woman, but knew that any move would halt her laughter quicker than anything.

"You have potential to be more than a catalog cowboy," she said finally, wiping the corner of her eye.

"Thanks, I think. What's a catalog cowboy?"

"Someone who orders all the appropriate gear from a catalog, but hasn't sat a horse or roped a steer."

"That wouldn't be me," Greg vowed, taking another sip of his coffee. "I have definitely ridden a horse before."

"Cutting? Roping? Western pleasure?"

"Eastern-riding-stable nag," he answered, hoping for another smile.

She didn't disappoint him. "I should have known."

Greg shrugged. "I don't have anything against horses. We just didn't have lots of them in our highrise condo when I was growing up." His family also owned a weekend house in the wooded countryside, but he didn't mention that detail, since they didn't have horses there, either.

"I don't suppose so," she admitted, reaching for a cookie. "I've heard the grazing on those small balconies is pretty scarce."

Greg laughed at the mental image of taking Puff

home with him to his Chicago apartment. "You could teach me to ride and rope," he said, leaning forward and resting his forearms on his crossed legs. "I'm a fairly athletic guy."

"I—" She obviously started to say something, then stopped herself. Her blush gave away her thoughts, though. She was remembering finding him by the pool yesterday. Like the rest of the conservative community, Ms. Carole obviously wasn't accustomed to seeing men in Speedos.

He wondered if she saw very many men *without* their Speedos. The thought wasn't nearly as easy to swallow as her cookies.

"Never mind. I probably won't be here that long," he said, mentally shaking away the thoughts of her with another man. "If you're ready, let me tell you a little about our company so you'll understand how important repairing our image is to the whole family, even the whole company."

"Okay," she said, setting her mug on the tray. "What did you have in mind?"

Greg finished his coffee, then set his mug beside hers. He leaned forward and clasped his hands. "You know Huntington Foods is an old, reputable company. My great-grandfather founded the firm in the 1920s, but really it grew in size by providing staple elements of the post-World-War-II American diet."

"As American as apple pie and cheese crackers."

"Exactly. And until my hotheaded older brother, Brad, the former C.E.O., decided to call a nutritional expert from C.A.S.H.E.W. a 'food nut' and appear to come at her across the table on national television, everything was going well."

"What happened to him? I couldn't believe the tape I saw on TV. It looked as though he snapped."

Greg shrugged. "The family is still debating that point, with my mother winning most of the arguments by blaming my father's Scottish ancestors. But at least he resigned quickly. Unfortunately, we still have a mess to clean up."

"Yes, but it's like a funny poster someone gave my sister, 'Poor planning on your part does not constitute a crisis on mine.'"

"That's a cute saying, and it might work fine if your job is stocking shelves at the grocery, or working as a clerk in the driver's license bureau, but that's not the same kind of situation you're in. I'm not sure how much of your income Huntington provides, but I do know how much we're paying you. That could take a big chunk out of your budget. If we can't get our image improved, sales of all our products, including your cookies, may suffer."

"Huntington has an obligation to pay me for my recipes."

"Not if we're forced to file bankruptcy."

She frowned, rubbing her arms with her hands in a nervous gesture. "The company is that badly off?"

"Not at the moment, but it's a possibility." Greg shrugged. "Brad appeared to be a loose cannon on national TV, giving the impression that the company is somewhat unstable." He leaned forward and looked into her eyes. "I can't think of a better person to re-form that image than you, a beautiful, intelligent woman who believes in having a plate of delicious cookies ready for her daughter when she comes home from school."

Carole rolled her eyes and chuckled. "You are some smooth-talkin' devil."

"Is it working?"

This time she laughed. "No, it's not." She leaned back and folded her arms over her chest. "Seriously...Greg," she said, hesitating over his name, "I didn't refuse to cooperate just to be difficult. I have my reasons for wanting to remain a private person."

"Does this have something to do with your daughter."

She paused, taking a deep breath that strained the buttons of her shirt, then said, "Jennifer is part of the reason, but no, not totally. Why can't you believe that someone would simply want to remain anonymous?"

"Because you really are my best, my only hope."

"I'm sorry, but I can't believe that's true."

"I'm being serious, Carole. Tell me why you don't want to promote your cookies. I know you believe in the product. I also know you are articulate, presentable and intelligent."

"Well, thank you for the compliments, but I really don't want to discuss my past with you."

He settled back against the couch and frowned. "I don't understand you."

She waved a cookie to emphasize her point. "Then stop trying. Just take my word for it—my past is in the past, where I want to keep it. The fact is that I made the deal I wanted with the company. They got what they paid for—my recipes—and I got what I wanted."

"Anonymity."

"And privacy. And no hassles from anyone asking me for favors."

"I'm not trying to hassle you. I'm just trying to save a company that's been in business since the twenties."

"I appreciate your dilemma, but I'm not the person you're looking for." Carole pushed up from the couch. "Excuse me for a moment."

Greg rose from his chair, reaching for the tray at the same time her hands closed over the handles. The surprise of touching her startled him as much as her reasonable responses to his explanations.

"Sorry," he murmured, looking across the tray into her eyes.

Her eyes widened, her hands slipping from beneath his as she stood up. "Never mind," she said. "I'll get it later. I'll be back in just a minute."

She nearly ran from the room. Greg stood beside the chair and watched her move, the worn denim cupping one of the nicest rear ends he'd ever seen. He told himself that looking at her *that way* was wrong. But he was in trouble. Personal trouble. At the moment he didn't know if he wanted Carole Jacks's cooperation on the Huntington Foods deal more than he wanted her naked in his bed. He hoped like hell he didn't have to make a choice between the two.

Like a kid with a tempting plate of Ms. Carole's confections, he wanted to have his cookies and eat them, too.

Chapter Four

Carole frowned at her complexion in the mirror. The cold water she'd applied to her hot cheeks had done little except make her look blotchy. No telling what Rafferty would think when she returned to the room. She looked positively ill.

As a matter of fact, her stomach was churning, but not from eating one cookie—or had she consumed two?—and drinking a cup of coffee. Her queasiness had been caused by the pseudo cowboy sitting in her living room as if he owned the place. He looked so darned comfortable, while she'd felt as skittish as a calf around a hot branding iron.

At least she'd lived up to her promise to Jenny; she'd listened patiently and with an open mind while Rafferty explained the situation. She'd been very reasonable, she told herself.

Folding the washcloth across the basin, she studied her reflection once again. The blotches were fading, being replaced by the usual slightly tanned glow she struggled to keep from getting any darker. Sunscreen was a must in Texas, and she used it by the quart. If she didn't keep her skin protected, she'd look like an old piece of tanned leather by the time she was forty.

"Like you're saving yourself for Mr. Right," she said to her reflection as she swiped some balm over her dry lips. "What difference does it make if you do look like a fifty-year-old saddlebag? You haven't kicked up your heels in a month of Sundays. How are you going to find someone special out here in the middle of nowhere if you don't go looking?"

She knew every eligible man for miles around, and the truth was, none of them tempted her to break her celibate lifestyle. Most of the men her age or slightly older were either married, engaged or good friends who sparked no romantic interest. A couple of years ago, some of the local matchmakers had fixed her up with Grayson Phillips when he first moved to town, but he'd been too suave and sophisticated for her.

The new architect and part-time rancher, Travis Whitaker, who was a good friend of Hank McCauley, was interesting, but she'd heard he was absolutely against getting married again after a nasty divorce. And she wasn't into casual affairs with people she might sit next to in church on Sunday or at a 4-H event next season.

Of course, all Mr. Greg Rafferty had to do was stroll into the county arena in his brand-new boots and jeans and she was ready to wrap herself around him like a prickly vine on a fence post. To think that he was sitting in her living room right now, all by himself...

"Darn it," she muttered, striding out of her bathroom, through the bedroom and into the hall. She'd left him alone too long. No telling what he was looking through. Her personal photos on the mantel. Her recipes in the kitchen. While she'd been dawdling, daydreaming about what was *never* going to happen, he could be stealing her newest cookie creation!

Sure enough, she found him in the kitchen, pouring coffee into their mugs.

"I thought you'd fallen in," he said with a smile as she strode into the room. "I hope you don't mind if I helped myself."

"To what?" she said, sudden anger making her tone peevish.

"Are you okay?" he asked, his tone concerned. He didn't seem to have a clue about why she was upset, but then, he could be acting innocent.

In keeping her promise to Jenny, and in nurturing her own attraction to a good-looking man, she'd overlooked the decisions she'd already reached. One, he'd proven he could be deceptive by trying to act the part of a cowboy, buying Puff on the pretense of saving him from Big Jim and feigning an interest in her to get her cooperation. Two, he was just too darned different from her for them to have anything in common. The fact they could carry on a conversation was practically a miracle.

"I'm fine," she said, stopping in front of her scribbled notes, still slightly dusted with flour. Well, at least he hadn't picked them up. And he probably hadn't been able to read them, she realized, because she had her own shorthand way of writing down quantities and ingredients.

"I think one Carole Jacks left the room and a different one came back in. There aren't alien pods in the other part of the house, are there? I think maybe the woman I was talking to minutes ago has been snatched." His tone sounded teasing, but she detected a note of concern in his voice, as if he thought she wasn't all that stable.

Of course she was stable. She was simply attracted to the wrong men.

"I haven't been snatched," she said crisply, the word bringing up images of *him* snatching her, whisking her away into the bedroom. Maybe she ought to consider being "snatched" by someone pretty soon, before her imagination kept pace with her darned raging hormones. Maybe Clive Perkins. He wasn't too bad, when he wasn't chewing. He had a nice body, too. Of course, he was just a little slow since he'd gotten kicked in the head by that Brahma bull last summer....

"Earth calling Carole," Rafferty said, waving a hand in front of her face. "I asked if you wanted anything in your coffee."

"Oh. Yes, sugar."

He handed her the bowl and a spoon, showing that he felt perfectly at home in her kitchen. The idea made her even more irritated, but she decided not to let it show. She'd already acted pretty snippy.

"Were you thinking about what I told you about Huntington?"

"Huntington? No, that's not what I was thinking about." She turned from his concerned gaze and cradled her mug in her two hands. "Let's sit down and finish our conversation."

"Of course, if you're sure you're feeling okay."

"I'm fine," she said emphatically, sloshing hot coffee onto her hand as she marched into the living room. "I'm just a little strung out today."

"Any particular reason? Other than my presence, of course."

She frowned at his quip, then took a deep breath as she sat down, carefully balancing her coffee. She wished she knew how to keep her personal and professional lives from spilling over into each other.

"I guess one reason is that Jenny is gone for the whole day, which reminds me that she's leaving next Monday for camp, and I'm going to miss her."

"Is this the first time she's gone away?" he asked as he took his seat in the chair.

"No. She loves summer camp, and she goes with some of the same kids each year, but that doesn't mean I don't miss her."

"Of course not. I'm sure you're very close."

Carole nodded, not exactly comfortable talking about this personal topic, even though speaking to Greg was somewhat easier than she'd anticipated.

"She's an only child, I take it?"

"Yes." And Carole knew that unless she did something drastic in the next few years, Jenny would stay an only child. Not that she was actively looking for a husband or more children. If the opportunity came up fairly soon, though, she would like to have a bigger family. Maybe a little boy to cuddle and tickle. Maybe a bigger "boy" to cuddle up with and... She had to stop thinking along those lines, especially with such a physically tempting specimen sitting in her living room. "How about you? Any little Raffertys back home?"

He laughed. "No. I've never been married, except to my job."

I've been married, she almost said, *for about two months.* She stopped herself in time. Her history wasn't his business. Johnny Ray French had been out of her life for more than ten years, which was just fine with her. When she looked back on her teenage stupidity—even though her bad decision had resulted in

Jenny, the joy of her life—she just wanted to cringe. She certainly didn't want to be reminded of her behavior by those sleazy tabloid journalists. She'd had enough of those when Kerry and Prince Alexi had been involved in their secret road trip and their rushed courtship last summer.

She especially didn't want Jenny to suffer because her mother, at age seventeen, hadn't possessed the sense of a cedar fence post. Carole hoped she'd gained some insight in the eleven years since she'd run away with the wrong guy.

"Are you ready to talk about the promotion ideas?"

She took a deep breath. "Look, Greg, I appreciate your position in the family business. I even understand why you think I'd make a good spokesperson, even though I know I wouldn't be your best choice. But I'm going to have to say no to your proposal."

"I haven't even told you the whole plan!"

Carole nervously turned away. "The answer is still no."

"Tell me this," he said, walking around so they once again faced each other. "Did you ever seriously consider becoming our representative?"

"I...I tried to keep an open mind."

"Did you?"

"Yes! Now I think it's time for you to leave."

He stared at her a long moment, then spun away. "I'm going, but we haven't finished this discussion."

"Yes, we have."

"You're not getting rid of me that easily, Ms. Carole," he said as he stalked toward the front door. "I didn't come all the way from Chicago to be blown off before you heard the whole plan."

"Why won't you just accept the fact that your plan and my lifestyle will never mix?"

"Because sometimes the best recipes are made from ingredients that seem to clash." He paused, his hand on the doorknob. "Kind of like you and me."

GREG DROVE AWAY from Carole Jacks's house, his knuckles white as he gripped the steering wheel. She was the most frustrating, stubborn and yet enticing woman he'd met in years. Maybe ever. Half the time he wanted to scream at his inability to make her see reason, and the other half he wanted to pull her into his arms and kiss her senseless.

Hell, *more* than half the time he wanted to kiss her senseless. And then some, he corrected as he turned from the rural route to the road that would take him into town. If he didn't believe she was nearly equally attracted to him, he'd never think about pursuing even a brief relationship.

He never pursued anything beyond brief, mutually exclusive relationships.

He'd boxed himself into a corner because he could only pursue his attraction to Carole if there was no way she'd agree to become the new symbol of Huntington Foods. Which meant he'd failed in his goal. He might as well pack up and go back to Chicago.

Except he had a twelve-hundred-pound steer who depended on him for two meals a day plus as many snacks as he could finagle.

The two-lane road bisected a dusty landscape of slightly rolling prairie land as he drove toward town. Green and dry brown grass hosted a few hardy wildflowers in yellow, red and pink. Limestone rocks pushed their way through the soil in uneven formations. Texas's fabled bluebonnets had apparently already faded now that summer was in full bloom. The scenery was vastly different from what Greg was accustomed to in Chicago, the surrounding area and the Lake Michigan summerhouse, yet he found the Hill Country landscape strangely compelling. He felt as if he was living a brief cowboy fantasy, complete with wide-open spaces and a pretty, feisty Texas cowgirl—who also baked cookies.

He pulled into a parking spot between the Four Square Café and Summers Real Estate office, across the street. A sign for the Prince Alexi Ladislas Museum beckoned visitors around the back of the building housing the café. What a strange attraction for a Texas town to host. Something in the news several months ago nagged at his conscience, but he couldn't quite recall why the prince's name seemed familiar.

His stomach rumbled as he walked past the plate-glass window to the door of the café. The cookies he'd eaten at Carole's house hadn't nearly satisfied his hunger, just as the short time they'd spent together had only whetted his appetite for more of her smiles and teasing comments.

More of *her.*

The bell attached to the heavy wood-and-glass door tinkled with old-fashioned charm as he stepped inside. The aroma of hamburgers, French fries and bacon filled the air. This was the café where Carole's mother worked, he knew. It was also the only true café in town, although there were a couple of fast-food places, a nicer "sit-down" restaurant and a new pizza place in town, he'd heard from Lester Boggs, the big talker who'd delivered Puff's feed.

"Well, hello there," an attractive, middle-aged lady said as she approached from the back. Her name tag simply read Charlene. "Just one?"

"Yes," he answered, "Mrs. Jacks."

She appeared startled for a moment, then smiled. "I guess you heard I work at the café. Well, I know who you are too, Mr. Greg Rafferty. You're giving my middle daughter fits."

Mrs. Jacks didn't appear too upset about that fact.

"Yes, ma'am, that I am," he said, grinning. "I would say I'm sorry, but I still think I'm right about needing her help."

"Carole can be very hardheaded." She settled a menu and a paper-napkin-rolled set of flatware on the paper placemat in one of the rear booths. "But then, each of my girls can be stubborn. That's one of their biggest assets...and more worrisome liabilities."

"I know what you mean."

"Well, I'm not sure about that, but I'll give you the benefit of the doubt." In an instant she changed demeanor from concerned mother to efficient waitress. "What can I get you to drink?"

"Iced tea would be great."

Greg sat with his back to the kitchen, giving himself an opportunity to look out at the café patrons and through the wide plate-glass window to the park-like town square. A white gazebo sat near this end. On the other side, some flowering trees—he thought they were called crepe myrtles—bobbed their heavily laden, deep-pink flowers in the slight breeze. Ranger Springs was a pretty little town...if one liked heat, wide-open spaces and stubborn cowgirls.

Maybe he should just give up on the idea of having Carole Jacks represent the company business, but she'd appeared so perfect, at least on paper. Her life and her aversion to publicity were a lot more complicated than he'd anticipated. He was accustomed to problems that could be solved with money, compromise or threats. None of those seemed to be working, although he had hopes for the "compromise" part of his standard solution.

Of course, if she wouldn't even listen to his plan, they'd never be able to compromise.

"Here's your iced tea. Have you decided?" Mrs. Jacks asked.

He hadn't even picked up the menu. "How about a cheeseburger and fries?" Every menu contained those staples.

"Everything on the side?"

"Sounds good." He smiled at Carole's mother, noticing the family resemblance. She appeared a lot closer in age to what he thought "Ms. Carole" should look like, but even the mother wasn't old enough for his initial image of Aunt Bea or Alice, the housekeeper. Did all the women in Texas look younger than their years, or did the Jacks family marry in their teens?

"Anything else?" she asked, cocking her head.

"No…just thinking."

"All right, then. Your lunch will be out in a few minutes."

"Thanks."

Maybe he should convince Carole Jacks that the best solution was to hire someone to portray her for the ads. That meant personal appearances limited to state fairs, cooking demonstrations on large stages and no interviews, but he could live with that if necessary. What he couldn't live with was failure.

And he really hated to give up, to admit defeat. He hadn't given up on his dreams for the past seven years, while his mother had been grooming his brother, Brad, to take her place as C.E.O. when she stepped down. Her illness had forced Brad into the position sooner than expected, which might have explained his outburst against the food police group, C.A.S.H.E.W.

If anyone in the family had asked him, Greg would have told them Brad was unsuited to the role of C.E.O. He didn't have any patience with any of the groups necessary to manage a large business, including labor, management and vendors. Brad was brilliant, but he needed to be his own boss, not be the boss of others.

His mother, who also had a stubborn streak a mile wide, had insisted Brad would grow into the job, that he just needed more time and training. She'd been wrong, unfortunately for Huntington Foods, although she'd finally come upon the obvious choice, Greg thought with no apologies for his own arrogance.

He'd wanted to be C.E.O. of Huntington Foods for as long as he could remember. Ever since his mother and father had taken him to the offices to visit his maternal grandfather, back when Pops had still been the head honcho. Greg remembered sitting in the big leather chair, still warm from his grandfather, and spinning around until the framed articles and plaques on the wall blurred together like an amusement park ride. In fact, he'd preferred Huntington Foods to the Navy Pier. He'd still rather watch the assembly line package crackers and cookies with the familiar hum and clank of heavy machinery than stroll along the boardwalk-like setting of Lake Michigan, eating cotton candy while carousel organ music filled the air.

Most people would say there was obviously something wrong with him, but he had no intention of fixing it. At least not until Huntington Foods was out of this crisis.

"Here you go, Mr. Rafferty."

Mrs. Jacks startled him out of his thoughts by placing a steaming cheeseburger and fries platter in front of him. The "nuts" at C.A.S.H.E.W. would have a mad fit.

"Please, call me Greg. And this looks and smells delicious."

"Since we're both in the food business, I suppose that's fine praise indeed. You enjoy your meal, Greg." Mrs. Jacks left for a circuit of the room, refilling iced tea glasses and coffee cups.

He'd only taken a couple of bites when a sixtyish gray-haired lady came up to his table. Intelligence and determination shone in her eyes. "Sorry to interrupt your lunch, but we met the other day at the arena, not that Carole introduced us. She was a little angry at you at the moment for buying Jennifer's steer."

"Ah, yes. You're the reporter."

"Thelma Rogers, owner, editor and reporter, too. I have a few part-time folks and some columnists who also write for the *Springs Gazette*."

Greg held out his hand and started to rise. "Greg Rafferty."

"Oh, don't get up. I just wanted to say hello and see if I could perhaps interview you about your stay in town."

"I'm not sure that would be a good idea. Carole Jacks is, as you said, a little irritated with me."

"Well, she's publicity shy, that's for sure. She won't ever let us sing her praises in the paper, afraid that someone from outside will pick up the story."

"What story?"

Thelma waved her hand. "Oh, any story. About how successful she's been with her cookie recipes. What a great mom she is to Jennifer by co-sponsoring the 4-H club. She even arranged for a fund-raiser to help supplement the purchase of animals for children whose parents couldn't afford them. She's a wonderful person."

"I'm sure she is. That's why I'm down here talking to her."

"Really?"

Afraid he'd told the newspaper owner and reporter more than he should have, he grimaced. "You aren't going to get a story about Carole out of me. She'd never forgive me for that blunder. I think I'm still in the doghouse for buying her daughter's steer and then *not* barbecuing him."

"Oh, I'm not planning a story about her. I was a lot more interested in why *you're* in town."

Greg folded his arms and gave Thelma Rogers his best corporate glare. "I'm here because of Carole Jacks, and that's all I'm going to say on the matter."

"So it's personal?"

"What part of 'that's all I'm going to say' didn't you hear?" he added with a smile to soften his words.

Thelma held up her hand and chuckled. "I understand. I'll stop prying."

"I'd appreciate it. The best I can promise is that if I have any news, I'll let you know first."

"That would be nice. Like I said, I'd never print anything that would harm Carole, her mother or her sisters. She felt bad enough after what we fondly call 'The Unfortunate Incident' years ago."

He sat up straighter. "What unfortunate incident?"

"Now that, Greg Rafferty," Thelma said with a shake of her finger, "is our secret. You have a nice lunch, you hear?"

Greg unfolded his arms and leaned back against the red vinyl booth. So much for enjoying his cheeseburger. What type of secret could Carole possibly be hiding?

Chapter Five

Although delving into the history of others wasn't
something he enjoyed, Greg decided he had no choice.
Carole wasn't going to tell him anything about her
past—she'd firmly refused to discuss her life outside
of the contractual obligations, except to mention her
daughter a few times: Jenny participated in 4-H; Jenny
went to camp every year. Not exactly groundbreaking
revelations. He'd have to dig deeper to understand
both Carole's aversion to expanding her role with
Huntington and Thelma Rogers's cryptic comment.

After pulling out his briefcase and locating the file
folder, he opened the report on Carole Jacks that
Huntington's legal department had run on her when
he'd first thought of her as a spokesperson. They rou-
tinely did background checks on potential employees
in key positions, so this wasn't unusual. However,
most people who underwent the background check
were applying for jobs.

Carole didn't want the job he'd offered. She didn't
want to have anything to do with him or his company
except supply them with recipes and receive a quar-
terly check.

His conscience only bothered him a little, since he

rationalized the research as necessary for saving his family business. If he convinced Carole to cooperate, he had to make sure she didn't have any skeletons lurking in her closet. No arrests or convictions that might be referred to by her friends and family as an "unfortunate incident."

Twenty-four hours a day his life revolved around one blond cowgirl. She had him tied in knots, and not just from her obvious physical attributes. She was also intriguing and admirable. Although she made him angry with her stubborn refusal to listen to his proposal to save Huntington's reputation, he believed she had her reasons.

He just needed to know those reasons.

He drummed his fingers on the desk as he read the report again. There simply wasn't much here. Carole didn't even have a traffic ticket or a misdemeanor on her record. She didn't have any alias or pending lawsuits, either. Her credit rating was excellent. The incident that Thelma Rogers had referred to obviously wasn't criminal.

She was as squeaky clean as her all-American good looks. So what was she hiding? Why was she so afraid of publicity?

The answer had to be something personal. Something had happened to her that didn't appear on any credit or criminal report. Something that made her wary of outsiders, afraid of placing herself and her daughter in the spotlight.

He flipped open his cell phone and called Stewart Allen, head of Huntington's legal department.

"Stew, we have a little problem down here in Texas." Greg briefly outlined his conversations with Carole, leaving out any of the personal stuff. He ended by mentioning his conversation with the newspaper lady. "I think we need a more in-depth investigation. Whatever has Ms. Jacks spooked is something personal. Something from her past. It may have to do with her ten-year-old daughter."

"I can get someone on it right away. We have a contract with a P.I. firm, although we seldom need their services."

"Good, because I sure wouldn't want to think we had to be this invasive into someone's privacy very often."

"I'm not sure how long this will take. Maybe a few hours, maybe a few days."

"I don't care as much about time as I do about discretion. I don't want any word of this investigation getting out. If Carole—Ms. Jacks, learned we were invading her privacy, there's no way in hell she'd ever agree to my plan."

"I understand. I'll call you as soon as I have something solid."

"Call me anytime. It's not like I have anything urgent going on down here in Texas, other than feeding my new pet."

"Pet?"

"Never mind. It's a long story. I'll talk to you soon."

Greg hung up the phone and leaned back in the chair. Several hours or several days, he really didn't have any plans. The only activity that interested him was strictly off-limits for several reasons, the most obvious one being that Carole Jacks had already asked him to leave her house once today. Going back would just be asking for more rejection.

He might be as stubborn as the mysterious cookie

queen, but he wasn't stupid. He wasn't about to screw up his only chance of making her see reason.

CAROLE PARKED behind the Four Square Café right at closing time. Her mother's car was parked beside the stairs leading upstairs to her beloved museum. Not that it was completely *her* endeavor. Since she'd been an ardent royal watcher for years and was now the mother-in-law to Prince Alexi of Belegovia, everyone called it "her" museum.

That was also one of the reasons Carole was now called the "cookie queen" when she'd previously been known as the "cookie mom," even though her older sister, Kerry, would one day be the queen of Belegovia.

After switching off the air-conditioning, then the engine, Carole quickly gathered the coffee cake and cookies she'd baked earlier. The café didn't get her baked goods every day, but she tried to keep them supplied on a regular basis. With Jenny gone all day and her encounter with Greg making her as jumpy as a cat in a roomful of rocking chairs, baking an extra batch or two of goodies seemed like a good way to work out her energy…and frustrations.

She knocked on the back door and was admitted by Hans, the cook. He was just tossing his apron in the dirty clothes hamper.

"Let me help you with that armload," he said, reaching for a couple of the containers.

"You're working late today."

"I was just leaving. We had a later than usual lunch crowd. Or I should say, they lingered longer than usual."

"Oh? Was there a Fall Festival meeting today?"

she asked as they walked into the kitchen with their loads.

"No, just a little gossip. A little talk about a certain out-of-town man you might know."

"Greg Rafferty?" she asked, her containers landing with a thud on the work island.

"The same. He was in earlier. Thelma talked to him, then she talked *about* him to the regulars."

Carole groaned. That meant Pastor Carl, Ralph Biggerstaff, Jimmy Mack Branson, Joyce Wheatley and maybe a couple of others had been discussing *her,* as well. Everyone in town was probably aware, by now, that an out-of-towner had paid three thousand dollars for Jenny's steer, even though he had no dinner plans for the animal.

Not very many men would pay that much for a steer unless he was trying to get into the good graces—or something—of the child's mother.

"Did they reach any earth-shattering conclusions?"

"Not that I heard. Of course, I was busy keeping them supplied with pie."

"I'm sure Mom will tell me," Carole said with a sigh. "Thanks for the warning, Hans."

"Sure thing. Thanks for bringing in the goodies. Your coffee cake is always a morning favorite."

"You're welcome. I'll see you in a couple of days with a fresh batch."

Carole walked down the tile hallway, past the stairs leading to the second floor, past the office, then the rest rooms and entered the main dining area. Her mother sat in the back booth, rolling flatware inside white paper napkins as she'd done for years.

"You should get someone else to do that, Mom," Carole said, settling into the bench seat across from

Charlene Jacks. She reached for a stack of napkins and moved the tray of knives, forks and spoons into the middle of the gray Formica table. She hadn't rolled as many napkins as her sister, Kerry, a former waitress who was now a princess in Belegovia, but she'd helped out enough to remember the routine.

"I know, but we're shorthanded at the moment. Darlene moved away, not that she was a lot of help, and we haven't been able to hire anyone else right now with school starting in a couple of weeks and everyone taking last-minute vacations."

Carole sighed, knowing her mother didn't like to participate in the interviews. She always fell for a hard-luck story and ended up recommending someone who wasn't suitable for waiting tables. Most people didn't realize what hard work was involved, from getting the orders straight to refilling coffee cups and glasses at just the right time.

"I heard Greg Rafferty was in earlier and that he talked to Thelma."

"She did most of the talking, if that's what you're worried about."

"I'm not worried," Carole said. "Well, not really. Of course I don't like the fact that he's made me the topic of idle conversation. I just wish he'd go back to Chicago. I don't understand why he's so certain he can make me change my mind when I've been very clear that I didn't want to cooperate with his plans."

"I don't know what to say, since you haven't told me what plans you're talking about," her mother gently chastised.

Carole stared at her blankly for a moment. "I thought I did. That's about all I've been thinking about for so long that I assumed...I'm sorry. I should have called and let you know."

"You don't have to let me know everything that's going on in your life, Carole Lynn. You're an adult."

"I know, but...if I'd thought that talking about him—I mean, his plan—would have helped, I'd have called you in a New York minute."

"So, do you feel like telling me why he's in town?"

"He wants me to represent his company, Mom. Huntington Foods. He had the gall to expect me to jump at the chance to be interviewed day and night, to have my home invaded by cameras and fly all over the country pushing plates of cookies at every local talk show host."

Her mother was silent for a moment, rolling the flatware, stacking the napkins. "Well, he obviously doesn't know you."

"That's for darn sure!"

"I suppose you told him no."

"Of course."

Her mother paused again, then asked, "Was there anything good about his plans?"

"No! Of course not. Oh, he offered me money. You know how those business executives are. They think throwing money at any problem will solve it."

"That's an unusual choice of words—problem. Is there a particular reason he wanted you to become Huntington's spokesperson?"

"You remember when Brad Rafferty, the former C.E.O., popped off to the food activist group on TV?" At one Saturday night family dinner they'd talked about his angry remarks, worrying that sales of Carole's cookies might suffer. Thankfully, they hadn't.

At her mother's nod, she continued. "Well, apparently the verbal battle has escalated to the point where Brad, who is Greg's brother by the way, had to resign and Greg is now stuck with rebuilding the company's image.''

''Then it seems reasonable he'd ask you for help.''

''He's not being reasonable! I have a contract that says I won't do any of the things he asked me to do.''

''Well, he didn't know for sure unless he asked.''

Carole narrowed her eyes at her mother. ''Whose side are you on?''

''Yours, of course, but that doesn't mean I can't point out the obvious. Greg Rafferty needs help, you're the logical choice, and he offered you money to cooperate.''

''Well, I'm not going to do it!''

Her mother nodded and continued to roll napkins. Sometimes she could be so...reasonable. Why wasn't she outraged that some Yankee had upset her daughter?

''I told him no, but he hasn't left. He doesn't believe I mean it, but I do. I swear, Mom, I'm not going to become a paid spokesperson for anyone.''

''I believe you, sweetie. And like you said, you certainly don't have to. You have a contract with Huntington Foods that pays you money without making you say one word on their behalf.''

''That's right! Now if Greg Rafferty would just get that through his thick head.''

Her mother sighed. ''You have to admit, he has a pretty darn good-looking thick head.''

''Mom!''

''I'm just stating a fact.''

Good thing her mother hadn't seen him in the Speedo, Carole thought. ''How attractive he is has nothing to do with the facts. He's been way too pushy. I don't appreciate him barging into my life, asking me to violate my principles, making Jenny giggle, for heaven's sake!''

"He sounds like he really needs help. That's probably made him a bit desperate.''

"Maybe, but that's his problem.''

"Of course it is.''

Carole frowned at her small stack of rolled-up flat ware. "Why won't he go away, Mom?''

"Because he hasn't gotten what he came here for.''

"He's never going to get my cooperation.''

"Then you don't really have a problem, do you, Carole Lynn?''

If only it were that simple.

JUST BEFORE SUNSET a very exhausted Jennifer arrived home from the amusement park in San Antonio. She waved wearily to her friends Ashley and Meagan while leaning against Carole's side. Still, she looked up with forced brightness and asked, "Can I go see Puff tonight?''

Carole hugged her warm little body close. "Not tonight, Jenny. It's late and you're tired.''

"Ah, Mom. I want to see him.''

But I don't want to see him, Carole felt like whining. *Him* being Greg Rafferty. She'd already seen him once today, and once was more than enough for her peace of mind.

"Not tonight, Jenny.''

"Can we go tomorrow?''

"Probably. I'll call Mr. Rafferty.''

"He'll want us to come out. He said I could come and see Puff anytime I wanted.''

Carole sighed. Talking to a ten-year-old who was physically exhausted would try the patience of a saint. "Are you hungry?" she asked, steering her daughter into the house.

"No. We ate hot dogs and nachos right before we left."

"Then let's get you into the bathtub."

"Ah, Mom," Jenny moaned, shuffling into the house like a condemned person.

"Into the tub, young lady."

While Jenny bathed and sang a pop song she must have heard on the radio today, Carole took out Greg Rafferty's impressively embossed business card. On the back he'd written his cell phone and the number at the house. His handwriting was neat and precise, not too small but not sprawling, either. Rather nice handwriting for a man, she had to admit.

She turned it over again and again between her fingers as if she were twirling a baton. *You have to call him sometime. Do it now. Then you can tell Jenny whether we'll be going over there tomorrow.* Before she chickened out, she picked up the phone and dialed his number.

"Rafferty here."

"Jacks here," Carole heard herself responding, wincing at the playfulness she heard in her own voice. Where had that come from? She was nervous. She didn't want to talk to him. Yet she found some humor in the situation? She must be as punchy tired as her daughter.

"Good evening, Ms. Jacks. It's nice to hear your voice."

"Thank you. I…that is, Jenny wanted to know if we could come by tomorrow and see Puff."

"Of course. He'll be glad to see Jenny."

"Good."

"And I'll be glad to see you."

She didn't know what to say to that remark. "What time would be convenient?"

"I have an early conference call to my office, but after around ten o'clock I should be free for several hours. Do you have time to talk while Jennifer visits her steer?"

"I'm not sure, and actually, he's your steer."

"Try telling him that. He still cries for her. It's very sad, really. I think I should send him home where he belongs. Just tell me when and I'll make arrangements with the feed store."

Carole chuckled. "That wasn't the deal."

"Do you have any idea how demanding a pet steer can be? It's like having a twelve-hundred-pound lapdog."

"Yes, I know exactly what you mean. Why do you think it was so hard for Jennifer to give him up, even for the sake of her college fund?"

"This whole 4-H thing seems rather barbaric."

"Only a Yankee city-slicker would make such a ridiculous comment. I'll bet you aren't even a vegetarian."

"No, I'm not, but I like to retain some space between myself and my meals. I haven't been able to eat any beef since Saturday without seeing Puff's big brown eyes staring at me. Condemning me."

Carole laughed. "Maybe you should become a vegetarian."

"I may start by eating only fish and chicken." He paused for a moment. "Jennifer doesn't raise pet chickens, does she?"

"No, but that's an idea for next year."

Greg Rafferty groaned. "So come by around ten o'clock. While Jennifer visits her big baby, we'll talk. I'll even make coffee."

Carole sighed. "You aren't going to leave this alone, are you?"

"I want to finish our conversation. I want you to give me a chance."

"I'm not changing my mind."

"Then help me come up with an alternative."

Would he really listen to her ideas? Did she even have any? Maybe she should think about his dilemma. After all, as her mother had pointed out, he must feel pretty desperate to come all the way to Texas, buy a steer, rent a house with acreage and keep pestering her to talk.

What man ever wanted to *talk?* From what she'd heard, a woman usually had to tie him up and threaten him with a cattle prod to get him to speak.

"Carole?"

Finally she said, "Make it iced tea and you've got a deal."

Chapter Six

Greg learned two things as he jogged down the rutted driveway, his lungs burning with the hot, dry air, every muscle screaming in protest. First, cowboy boots were not meant for extended walking, much less running. Second, big, overgrown steers could run a lot faster than he'd ever imagined.

He'd been a little late feeding the huge baby because he'd spent a mostly sleepless night thinking about Carole. About what those curve-hugging jeans concealed...and what personal information she might be hiding. About how she'd called him last night to ask about coming over...and how he'd wanted to talk about so much more than business.

And after his mostly sleepless night, he'd barely had time for a cup of instant coffee before his conference call, so he hadn't gone out to feed the big black beast until almost ten o'clock. At which point he'd seen the steer's wide rear end and wavy-hair-tipped tail disappear down the driveway.

"I need a horse," he wheezed, stopping to bend slightly and rest his hands on his knees as Puff veered off the drive and cut across the wide-open spaces. A cross-country motorcycle would be good. Or even one of those sissy little scooters. Anything but jeans and boots for chasing cows.

Being a cowboy was a lot harder than he'd anticipated. He couldn't explain to an animal why talking about a new contract for shipping their baked goods was more important than ten pounds of grain and fresh water. He couldn't even apologize to the dumb beast for being late. All he could do was chase him down and hope that Puff would let himself be led all the way back to the pasture by his halter.

Greg realized, now that it was too late, that he should have brought a lead rope.

He stumbled on a clump of grass, then struggled to right himself just as he heard the sound of crunching gravel. Sure enough, Carole and Jennifer were right on time. He groaned as he straightened, half hoping they didn't see him, but knowing he needed help more than he deserved to salvage his pride.

Carole veered toward him across the unfenced pasture, her truck bouncing across the uneven ground. He shaded his eyes and looked inside. Jennifer was pointing beyond him, to where Puff meandered around, looking for more trouble, no doubt. Carole appeared intense. Maybe a little angry. He sure as hell hoped she didn't plan to run him over with her truck. Losing her daughter's prize steer might make her a little testy. Not that she needed much of a reason to dislike him, he reminded himself.

At the last minute she steered to the side and came to a dusty stop. Leaning out the window, she asked, "What in the world are you doing?"

Before he could answer, she sped off again, leaving him covered in more dust as she chased down the steer. With a sigh, he limped after the truck. Despite her more friendly tone last night on the phone, her opinion of him obviously hadn't improved. Not that he really blamed her. He was sure that to a native Texan who grew up around cowboys, seeing someone limping after a runaway steer looked pretty odd.

He watched Jennifer fling open the door and jump to the ground as soon as the truck came to a stop closer to Puff. She placed two fingers in her mouth and whistled, a surprisingly loud sound coming from such a little girl. Puff stopped his forward motion, then turned his head to look at the person who raised him. With a happy bellow, the steer turned around and trotted back to Jennifer, just like a well-mannered puppy.

"If only I'd known how to whistle," Greg complained as his boot rubbed another blister the size of Texas on his heel.

CAROLE PLACED HER HANDS on her hips and glared at Greg. "I can't believe you took off on foot to chase down a steer."

"He didn't seem to be going very fast at first," he replied, wincing as he tried to pull off his boot, one leg crossed over his other knee.

Carole shook her head. He probably had some really nasty blisters. No telling what kind of socks this city-slicker wore with his Tony Lama boots.

"Here, let me," she offered gruffly. There was no sense in watching him suffer through his current silliness. Chasing a steer on foot! Only someone who'd grown up in the city would do such a fool thing.

"What?"

"Stick your leg out straight."

As soon as he complied, she swung one leg over his extended one, facing his foot. Of course, this gave him an excellent view of her worn jeans, which were relatively threadbare over her bottom, but she couldn't do anything about that for the moment. Besides, he seemed to be able to control himself around her. After all, he wanted her cooperation with his company. He might be slightly interested in her as a woman, but he was a lot more intent on her as a potential spokesperson for Huntington Foods.

"Er, Carole, what are you doing?"

Doing? She was daydreaming, of course. "Just sit still, relax your foot, and I'll have this boot off in a second." She grasped the sole and the heel and pulled off the boot in a rolling motion guaranteed to cause the least amount of discomfort.

"Ouch!"

"Don't be a baby," she scolded mildly, placing the boot on the floor. "Give me your other foot."

When he didn't immediately respond, she swiveled around to glare at him. "Hey, I don't have all day here."

His gaze snapped to her face. He'd been staring at her rear end! Why, of all the ungrateful... But then she felt a little warmed by the fact he'd been staring at her. As if he liked what he saw. As if he couldn't help himself.

She kind of liked that feeling of power. However, she'd never let him know how she felt. Forcing a frown, she ordered, "Other foot, Rafferty, and make it quick."

He drew his leg back, his denim rubbing against her denim in a way that made her think of other reasons their body parts might be sliding back and forth. Suddenly his kitchen seemed way too warm, just like their position seemed way too intimate.

"Be gentle with me," he said, sliding his other foot between her legs.

She grasped his foot and tried not to think about all the ways she could take that remark. "In your dreams," she answered gruffly, jerking off the boot with a little more force than absolutely necessary.

"Ouch! Again! I think you're enjoying this torture."

"Like that old saying, If the Shoe Fits. Or maybe I should say 'boot.'" She let go of his foot and stepped away, turning quickly to face him. She didn't want to encourage him to stare at her butt. Not really. That would be juvenile, vain and petty, since they weren't going to have any sort of personal relationship.

"Very funny."

"What?" Had he heard her thoughts?

"That remarks about 'if the shoe fits.' What did you think I meant?"

"Nothing. I'd just moved on. Now, about those blisters…" He'd mentioned them when he'd climbed into the truck for the short ride back to the house while Jenny led Puff back to the pasture.

"I have blisters on my blisters."

"You're a big baby."

"My boots are new."

"You're not required to wear them all the time just because you're cooling your heels in Texas for who knows how long. Until you come to your senses, I suppose."

"'Cooling my heels' is not the operative term. I feel like they're being broiled, not chilled."

"Let me look."

"You don't have to play nursemaid."

"I'm not playing. I'm a mom. I'm pretty good at patching up minor cuts and scrapes."

"I think this is major."

She laughed at his typically male response to a little pain. She'd always thought it was strange that guys could complain like crazy over a hangnail, but remain stoic and in denial over things like broken arms and dislocated shoulders. Especially if they got those injuries doing guy things, like rodeo, football or major home improvements. She'd observed this phenomena in Hank McCauley and several other friends. She'd also heard stories about her friends' husbands that had her rolling on the floor.

She wished she'd had the experience from her own father, but he hadn't stuck around long enough for her to remember any humorous incidents from their time together. And she and her husband—her brief teenage fling—hadn't been together long enough to know anything beyond burning up the sheets, eating fast food and dreaming about "making it big someday."

She sighed away the dark thoughts. "Take those socks off and let's see what you've done to yourself."

"The boots did it, not me," he said as he pulled off the white athletic socks. At least he'd worn something sensible with his boots instead of those thin, sissy socks like some businessmen wore with their suits. Of course, she had a problem visualizing Greg Rafferty in a suit. He'd worn nothing but casual Western wear since he arrived in Ranger Springs.

Why was that?

"Yep, that's pretty bad," she said after seeing the red, blistered areas of his heel. "Next time, don't run around in boots. These are ropers, made to settle into the stirrup real nice and give you some leverage for when the horse comes to a quick stop. Not made for running after steers.''

''Yeah, I'll try to remember that,'' he said, poking at one of the blisters. ''Can you fix these?''

''Not really. I can put some antibiotic ointment on them, then cover it with a light bandage. Don't worry. The blisters will go away in a few days.''

''A few days! I can't go around barefoot for days.''

''I don't know what to tell you.''

Greg narrowed his eyes, then smiled at her. ''Since Jennifer's steer caused the problem, I think maybe you owe me.''

''*Your* steer caused the problem, and no, I don't owe you anything.''

''But you're my only friend in town, and I could really use some help.''

He said that line with such sincerity in his heavily lashed, blue-green eyes that Carole almost melted. Almost. ''If I'm your only friend, you have more problems than a couple of blisters.''

He laughed, a deep, throaty sound that made her breath catch. ''Come on, Carole. Be nice. I need to buy some more clothes. Some sandals with no back strap so I can walk around without pain. Maybe some tropical print shirts and baggy cotton shorts to go with them, since my new jeans or my old chinos are going to look a little strange. Is there a men's clothing store in town?''

''Not like you're obviously used to. We have one of those big discount centers out on the highway. You could probably get an entire wardrobe for what you usually pay for one shirt.''

''Hey, I'm not a snob. I'll take what I can get.''

"I can't believe you realized that sandals wouldn't look good with your existing clothes."

He shrugged. "What can I say? Appearances are important."

Carole sighed again. Greg was intent on pulling her into his life, one way or another. Not that he'd planned to run after Puff in a pair of boots. He just seemed to turn every challenge into an opportunity to spend more time with her. To bring her around to his way of thinking.

Well, she wasn't changing her mind just because he'd started to get under her skin. Just because he was attractive and sexy and had a good sense of humor. Just because he turned lemons into lemonade. Just because he was consistently nice to Jenny, even when her steer ran off and caused him problems.

"Oh, okay. But I'm driving."

"That's fine with me. I have nothing against women drivers."

She called for Jenny, who'd fed and groomed Puff, and they all got cleaned up from their dusty morning activities. Before long they were headed for her pickup. Only then did she realize what a mistake she'd made.

Unlike some of the newer, more expensive models, her pickup only had one bench seat. No extended cab with a rear seat. She, Jenny and Greg would be pressed together.

He grinned, obviously because the dilemma was reflected on her face. She'd never been good at poker.

"Jenny, you sit in the middle."

"Ah, Mom. You know I get car sick if I can't see out."

"You can see out the front."

"I want to see out the side, too. Just in case I feel a little queasy."

Darn it, why was Jenny being difficult? She'd sat in the middle before when her friends rode with them. She couldn't be playing matchmaker, could she? Surely not at age ten!

"Hey, I don't mind sitting in the middle," Greg offered.

I'll just bet you don't, Carole felt like saying, but she kept her mouth shut. One thing she'd learned in the past few days was that she rarely got in the last word around Greg Rafferty.

GREG SAT in the middle of the bench seat, both arms casually outstretched along the back. On Jennifer's side, he kept his hands on the seat back. On Carole's side, however, he let his hand drop occasionally to her shoulder. Or to brush the back of her spun-gold hair. She invariably stiffened, sometimes glaring at him, but she didn't say anything. He had her daughter to thank for that. Apparently Carole didn't want to make a scene she'd have to explain later to the ten-year-old.

He also let his bare thigh gradually drift against Carole's leg, lightly brushing her jeans until she noticed. At first she'd glare at him and try to move away—a difficult feat since she needed to use that foot for driving. But the last time he'd "accidentally" brushed against her, she'd done the unexpected. She'd used her leg, her knee whopping against his thigh, a lot more surprising than painful. He grinned and dropped his hand to her shoulder again. Feeling her denim-clad leg against his had reminded him of when she'd pulled off his boots, which was one of the most memorable experiences of his recent life. She had a great rear end and absolutely enticing thighs. He'd had to concentrate on the pain of his blisters to keep from running his hands up her legs, pulling her onto his lap and kissing her neck.

Sitting next to her in the truck was only slightly less tempting, but at the same time, it was kind of fun. She drove while he got to "play." And chat with Jennifer, too, as she pointed out landmarks like the turnoffs to her friends' houses, a shortcut to a neighboring town, or a hidden favorite swimming hole. Jennifer was cute and charming, much like her mother must have been at that age.

"Are we there yet, *Mom?*" Greg asked, eliciting a giggle from Jennifer. Since dressing down in clothes he usually reserved for working out, he felt a bit more playful than usual. He didn't think the cotton knit shorts and sweatshirt with the sleeves cut off would be out of place in the discount store.

"Thankfully," she answered, shrugging off his wandering hand, "we're almost there. Just around the next curve."

They pulled into one of those big supercenters Greg avoided, just as he stayed away from children's movies and teen music concerts. But perhaps with Carole and Jenny, the experience wouldn't be too bad.

Thirty minutes and a shopping-cart load of clothes, bandages, pain-killing antibiotic spray and various other items he couldn't live without, he had to admit he'd had a pretty good time. While the clothes he'd selected weren't his usual style, Carole and Jennifer seemed to like them. Especially the tropical print shirt with the pink flamingos. He had a suspicion they were setting him up, but seeing their smiling faces was worth whatever embarrassment might follow.

He also insisted on buying a treat for Jennifer because she'd retrieved Puff with such ease, and for Carole for removing his boots and doctoring his blisters.
The ten-year-old picked out a favorite pop-rock CD
she'd been waiting for, but Carole was a little harder
to convince. Finally, after several "silly" suggestions
including a new baking sheet for cookies and a racy
nightgown that raised everyone's eyebrows, she se
lected a box of chocolate-covered cherries she grudgingly admitted were a rare treat.

Jennifer gave a hearty "uck." Greg raised his eyebrows again, definitely having more naughty fantasies
about Carole's secret indulgences. And what he could
do with those candy delights, a little candlelight and
some silky smooth sheets.

*Not if you want her agreement to represent
Huntington Foods,* he reminded himself. He found
himself thinking more and more about Carole, the
woman, than Ms. Carole, the potential spokesperson.
Especially today, after she'd taken care of him and his
shopping needs.

He paid for his purchases with a personal credit
card. It wasn't Huntington's fault he'd lost the steer
and chased him across the countryside.

"Since we're already out, why don't I buy us some
lunch?" Greg said as they tossed their purchases in
the bed of the pickup.

"Great!" Jennifer responded immediately, opening
the passenger door.

"I'm not sure that's a good idea," Carole said almost as quickly.

"Aw, Mom."

Greg slid across the bench seat and smiled at Carole

as she opened the other door. "Yeah. Aw, Mom. Come on. We'll have a good time."

"I have things to do." She slid in beside him.

"I won't keep you long. Besides, you have to eat, right?"

"We could go see Grandma," Jennifer pointed out.

He felt Carole shudder as she gripped the wheel. "I'm not sure that's a good idea."

"I met your mother. She's very nice."

"Having lunch at the Four Square Café is not a good idea," Carole insisted as she turned the key and started the engine.

"Why not?" Jennifer asked. "I like the food there. Not as much as McDonald's, but it's good."

Greg laughed. Carole leaned forward, peering around him to frown at her daughter. "Don't let Grandma hear you say that."

Jennifer giggled. "Come on, Mom. It'll be fun."

SHE KNEW this wasn't going to be a good idea. Unfortunately, Greg had used Jenny to overrule good sense. Two against one. And Carole wasn't accustomed to having her daughter side with someone else against her.

She watched Jenny, sitting next to Greg Rafferty, laughing as he charmed Charlene Jacks. Carole's mother was smiling, looking much younger than she had in months. Everyone was having a great time. Even the regulars at the café were watching the happy family, smiling as they took in the scene. Mother, daughter, grandmother…and good-natured scoundrel.

Darn it, he was doing it again. Wheedling his way into her family's good graces, acting like the perfect gentleman, the absolute charmer. Everyone was eating out of the palm of his hand. Everyone except her. Was she the only person who knew he was doing all this for a reason? That he wasn't as wonderful as her daughter, her mother—and probably much of the town—thought he was?

As Thelma joined them and beamed at Greg, Carole suspected the answer to her question was yes. She *was* the only person who knew the real, succeed-at-all-costs, hard-edged businessman who lurked beneath that cut-off sweatshirt, cotton shorts and sports sandals.

She didn't have much of an appetite after watching Greg's performance at the café. And also after enduring his casual touches during the ride to and from the store. The man was like an octopus, except a very teasing, playful one. She'd been out with men—boys, really—who did a lot more groping than Greg. He had a real finesse to his style, making the contact so casual, sometimes so seemingly innocent, that she couldn't just come out and swat his hand away. Especially not with Jenny in the truck, taking in everything, even things that at ten years of age, she didn't understand.

Man/woman things. Things she'd never had to deal with because her mother didn't have relationships. There had been no boyfriends to worry about introducing to her daughter, no "uncles" that spent the night. At times Carole was really proud of her lifestyle, focusing on her daughter and family, but at other times, her lack of a personal life seemed pretty pathetic.

She could barely remember what she was missing. Teenage sex, filtered through memories of teen angst, had seemed exciting, forbidden and urgent. Not especially enjoyable, however. Johnny Ray had been only nineteen, and although he'd been with a few other girls, he didn't know all that much, she suspected. At least, not compared to the men she read about in books and watched in the movies.

Now Greg Rafferty…there was a man who probably knew what a woman wanted. What she needed.

Not that *she* needed what Greg had offered. And not exactly that he'd offered it, come to think of it. Or had he? She felt so confused.

"Are you hot, sweetie?" her mother asked as she placed iced tea in front of the adults plus a lemonade for Jenny.

Her mother's voiced jolted her back to awareness. She was sitting inside the Four Square Café, not in some dark motel room. Not in the back seat of a car. And definitely not doing the wild thing with Greg Rafferty.

"It is a little warm in here, isn't it?" she answered, dabbing at her forehead with her napkin.

Greg smiled, almost as if he knew what she'd been thinking. She sincerely hoped that her thoughts weren't that easy to read. If so, she was in serious trouble.

She was saved from further comment when Travis Whitaker walked in. Carole knew he was an architect, but he'd taken to ranching with ease, settling on land adjacent to Hank McCauley's spread a couple of years ago when he tired of the city. He still traveled quite a bit, accepting only those jobs he really wanted. She'd heard he took lots of vacations, too, usually with a trophy girlfriend. Rumor was he didn't date anyone very long and had no intention of getting serious.

His life sounded like a lot of fun. Too bad she didn't feel any sparks when she looked at him. A nice tropical vacation with no strings attached sounded pretty good sometimes. Not that she'd actually go....

"Hi, Thelma, Charlene. How are you, Jennifer, Carole?"

"We're just fine, Travis. Would you like to join us?" she asked, scooting over. Maybe having another man around would keep Greg from charming everyone so easily.

"Maybe just for a few minutes. I'm meeting Hank and Gwendolyn to talk about horses."

"You're getting into cutting horses?" Carole asked.

"No, but I thought I'd upgrade my stock, now that I've learned to ride with a little more skill. Maybe get a couple of mounts with more training and spirit. I still need a few horses that are nice and calm for when my niece and nephew come to visit."

"I could have used a horse this morning," Greg commented. "I felt like that scene from *Richard III*. 'A horse, a horse, my kingdom for a horse.'"

Everyone laughed, and Carole smiled at the memory of Greg painfully loping across the field after Puff. So much for him being less charming with a little competition for attention.

Greg explained to Travis, "Jennifer's steer thought I wasn't going to feed him breakfast, so he broke out of the pasture and went after it on his own."

"Mr. Rafferty was really funny, Grandma, chasing Puff across the field."

"Now, Jennifer, it's not nice to laugh at someone else," Carole's mother gently chastised.

"It's okay, Mrs. Jacks. I'm sure I looked pretty funny. At the time, all I could think about was catching Jennifer's steer."

"He's *your* steer now," Carole pointed out.

Everyone seemed to ignore her. "That's so sweet," Thelma said.

Carole rolled her eyes while Travis chuckled and Jenny giggled. She knew coming to the Four Square Café for lunch wasn't a good idea.

And she'd already promised Greg that she would talk to him today about ideas for saving Huntington Foods. Would he hold her to that promise after all the excitement of this morning? Or would she get a reprieve so she could remind herself that he wasn't really as charming and sincere as everyone else thought?

Chapter Seven

"Is it too late to have our talk now?" Greg asked as Carole pulled the truck to a stop in front of his house. After all, they had planned to talk at ten o'clock this morning, and they'd spent the past three hours together doing everything but discussing Huntington Foods' problems.

"Well…I had planned on getting some work done this afternoon," she said, putting the gear in park but not turning off the engine.

"And don't forget, Mom, that I have a sleepover tonight at Ashley's house and you promised to bake cookies," Jennifer said, leaning around Greg so she could look at Carole.

"Oh, yes. I had forgotten." Carole looked at him and shrugged. "I do have some other commitments."

"You aren't trying to get out of our talk, are you?"

"Of course not. I made a promise, and I'll stand by my word."

"Good, because I really do want to hear your ideas."

"What ideas?" Jennifer asked.

He turned to smile at the girl. "About making people like Huntington Foods better so they'll buy more of your mom's cookies.''

"Oh. How come your family owns the company and your name's not Huntington?'' she asked.

"Because my mother's name was Huntington before she married my father. His name is Rafferty, so now the Raffertys are running the company.''

"That's kind of like my mom, except we got to use her name instead of my dad's because he's not really my dad like other dads who live with their family. But that's okay because we're all Jacks instead of me being a—''

"Jenny, I don't think Mr. Rafferty will find our family history very interesting.''

He turned back and smiled at Carole. "On the contrary, I find it fascinating.''

Carole glared at him.

"My mom and dad got married, then got 'nulled.''

"Annulled,'' Carole corrected. "And that's enough family history, young lady.''

Very interesting, he thought as Jennifer opened the car door and hopped out. So Carole married Jennifer's father, but they didn't stay married long enough to warrant a divorce. Or was the annulment story just that? Had she really married the guy? Maybe she'd never been married but didn't want her daughter to know.

He scooted across the bench seat as hot air filled the truck's interior from the open door. Was a rushed annulment the "unfortunate incident" Thelma Rogers had referred to, or were there more secrets in Carole Jacks's past?

Jennifer gave a dramatic sigh as she stood outside, then asked, "Will you be able to feed Puff his dinner,

Mr. Rafferty? I could come back over if you need me to."

"I think I can manage," Greg answered, hopping down to the gravel. "I'll remember to feed him on time."

"Mom could come by when she takes me to the sleepover. Then you could talk about ideas."

Greg didn't comment that Carole would be welcome anytime for their own personal sleepover. He had enough ideas for both of them. "That would be great. What do you say, Carole?" he asked, turning back to look inside the truck. "Do you have time to stop by later to talk? I still owe you an iced tea."

"It's been a long day," she said, hedging.

"Yes, but we could sit down and relax. Have a cool drink and try to figure out what's best for all of us." He paused, placing his hands on the roof of the truck and leaning inside just slightly. "I could really use your advice on how to proceed. After all, my family's company is still in trouble."

He could tell she was wavering by the sympathetic look in her eyes, combined with a worried, I-don't-want-to-be-alone-with-you expression that reminded him how he'd playfully flirted with her all day. The challenge of making her aware of him as a man while they were in public or riding in her truck, her daughter sitting next to him, gave him an adrenaline rush. That must explain why his libido kept overriding his good sense. No matter how often he told himself that Carole was more important as a spokesperson than as a romantic interlude, he kept thinking of her smooth, lightly tanned skin, blond hair and sparkling eyes. He kept hearing her slightly husky, Southern-accented voice, and he wanted her to be his. His *what,* he wasn't sure.

Around Carole, an urge more primitive than his business education or goals guided his words and gestures at times, which was a new experience for him. He'd always thought of himself as someone in complete control of his actions. He'd always known that he wouldn't achieve his goals by goofing off and proving to his parents that he wasn't fit for the job he'd always wanted.

Now he'd gotten what he'd wanted, but he kept forgetting his position with the company when he started thinking about all the positions in which he'd like to get Carole. With her complete cooperation and enthusiastic response, of course.

"I suppose I could stop by around seven o'clock this evening."

"Great. I'm really looking forward to seeing you later." And because that sounded too much like a date, he added, "To discuss your ideas." He moved away from the open passenger door.

"Yes, of course," she said, appearing almost as flustered as he felt. "Seven o'clock," she repeated as Jennifer jumped up on the seat, gave him a smile and waved goodbye.

ONCE AGAIN Carole debated about what to wear. How to wear her hair. Whether she should take cookies to their "meeting," as she preferred to call the discussion she and Greg would have tonight. It definitely wasn't a date, even though the time was evening and they would not be chaperoned by a ten-year-old busybody who thought nothing of telling strangers the family secrets.

Okay, maybe Greg Rafferty wasn't a stranger, and maybe Carole's early marriage to Johnny Ray wasn't exactly a secret, but still, Jenny shouldn't just blurt out her mother's marriage history to anyone. Especially to people—like Greg—who seemed exceptionally interested in her past, present and future, Carole thought as she laid out yet another change of clothes on her bed. She'd already discarded the idea of wearing a T-shirt and overalls, or white shorts and a red striped top, or yet another pair of blue jeans.

Thank heavens the paparazzi weren't hanging around any longer. No telling what they'd learn from Jenny, she thought with a shudder. When Kerry had married Prince Alexi, the whole family had kept Jennifer, who had been nine at the time, away from prying eyes and pushy reporters who wanted to find something naughty and juicy to report in their rags.

Carole knew that keeping her daughter isolated at age ten would be a heck of a lot harder. Which gave her even more reason not to become a public figure. She had no right to put her daughter into the position of either lying to protect their privacy or accidentally letting something slip that could be considered scandalous.

No, Jenny was a lot happier in her current life than she would be as the daughter of a celebrity. Some people might think that since her friends and neighbors knew she was the Carole behind Ms. Carole's cookies, she was already semifamous, but that just wasn't true. No one thought anything of the fact she'd licensed her recipes to Huntington Foods. They were a lot more excited when she donated cakes to the church bake sale or tried out a new recipe at the Four Square Café. To them, Huntington Foods was a big, northern-based company that didn't have much relevance in their daily lives. A good coffee cake or batch of chocolate chip cookies—now that was something to get excited about!

Carole smiled as she assessed the latest outfit she'd chosen, a short but modest denim skirt and a peasant-style blouse that was cool and comfortable. She'd worn these clothes out in public before, so no one should think they were special. Or assume she was dressing up for Greg Rafferty. Which she wasn't, of course. She just wanted to be at ease for her meeting with the smooth talker from Chicago.

Decision made, she quickly dressed, then brushed her hair until it fell smooth and straight, tucked behind her ears. She added a pair of dangling silver earrings her sister Cheryl had given her and slipped her feet into some simple sandals with a small heel. Looking down, she wiggled her toes. Good thing she'd given herself a pedicure the other night.

That would have been the night she couldn't sleep because she was thinking about Greg Rafferty.

"You look nice, Mom," Jenny said from the doorway, jerking Carole's thoughts back to the present.

"Thanks, honey. It's so hot that I wanted to be comfortable."

"My friends would say *you* look hot," her precocious ten-year-old said with a cheeky grin.

"Quit teasing your old mother and get your overnight bag."

"You're not old. You're not even thirty yet. All the other mothers are older."

That's because I ran away and got married when I was only seventeen, Carole wanted to say. *And don't make the same mistake!*

But how could she ever call her teen marriage a mistake when she'd conceived Jenny? At eighteen, single and pregnant, she hadn't felt very lucky. But she'd soon held her baby in her arms and fallen in love with the little imp. Now she couldn't imagine life without Jenny.

A few minutes later they were in the truck and on their way to Ashley's house. With every mile they drove, Carole's trepidation increased. Maybe she shouldn't have agreed to see him again tonight. The timing was all wrong. They'd practically spent the day together.

She'd removed his boots, for goodness' sake! She'd held his foot in her hands, then later batted away his wandering leg while they were driving around. He sat right there, she remembered, glancing at the middle of the black tweed seat cover, and flirted with her in front of Jenny. Okay, maybe he wasn't really flirting, but he was teasing her with his nearness. Overwhelming her senses with his presence. Too close. Too male.

She didn't know how to react to a man she was attracted to. She didn't know how to interpret his signals. Was he seriously attracted to her, or did he treat all women this way? She'd tried to tell when they were in the café, but she'd been too worried about other things. Like how he was taking over the conversation, charming everyone. She didn't know him well enough to know what to believe about him, and she wasn't sure she wanted to get to know him well.

She pulled to a stop in front of the rambling ranch-style brick home of Ashley's parents. "Be polite and don't stay up too late," Carole advised, shifting automatically into "mom" mode.

"Okay, Mom. I'll call you in the morning when it's time to leave. I might get a ride home with Meagan."

"That's fine, but let me know so I won't worry."

"Okay," Jenny said, leaning over the plate of cookies for a kiss.

Carole hugged and kissed her baby, then watched her rush into the house, overnight bag bumping against her still-girlish hips, long brown braid flying. She sighed. Soon her little girl would become a young woman. She wasn't ready. She might never be ready for those teen challenges. She hoped Jenny had more sense than she had as a teen. Carole wondered how her mother had survived all the trouble she'd caused by running off, getting married and coming home alone and pregnant.

But Jenny didn't know about that part of the family history. She accepted the fact her father wasn't a part of their lives, although she sometimes wished she had a real dad. Carole wished she could have provided a real father to her daughter, just as she wished Jenny had a grandfather. But wishing wasn't going to provide the strong male influence that many books said was necessary for girls. All Carole could do was provide opportunities to be around men on a temporary basis, like Hank McCauley, who'd always been a good friend, before and after he'd dated Kerry. Even now, after marrying Lady Gwendolyn, he still included the Jacks family in barbecues, horseback rides and other gatherings at his ranch. And Gwendolyn, who was the daughter of an English earl, had become a surrogate aunt to Jenny.

But enough of her musings, she thought, putting the truck into gear. She had made a commitment to Greg Rafferty to discuss his company's problems. She drove away from Ashley's house before she thought of any excuses to stay away from the smooth-talking businessman.

GREG FELT as nervous as a college kid who'd scored a date with the homecoming queen. His palms grew damp as he placed napkins on the coffee table next to two sweating glasses of iced tea. He then lined up the two spoons next to a sugar bowl, hoping he'd thought of everything.

Hoping Carole showed up, he thought, frowning at the clock on the wall. Five minutes after seven. Had she decided she didn't want to speak to him about his family's business? Had something else come up, something she'd rather do than talk to him?

Just when he'd decided pacing was the only answer, he heard her truck crunch the gravel of his driveway. Striding to the door, he breathed a sigh of relief. As long as she was willing to talk, he had a chance to convince her to become Huntington's spokesperson.

He wasn't sure what he'd do if she decided not to discuss the issue anymore. At that point he'd probably pack up and go home to Chicago. Come up with another plan. And try to forget Carole, the woman, even as he gave up on Ms. Carole, the cookie queen.

She parked facing the house, then pushed the door open. One shapely leg descended, then another. Instead of her usual jeans and boots or athletic shoes, she wore something short with sandals. The truck's door hid most of her from view, but still, his breath caught.

Then she pushed it shut and he got his first glimpse of the whole woman. Wow. She looked better than any homecoming queen he'd ever seen. Dressed in one of those soft, sort of hippie-looking blouses that tied in front and a short denim skirt, she appeared too young to be a mom. Too sexy to be a spokesperson.

If she went along with his plans, he'd have to dress her in body-hiding suits with high necks and low hems. Not that *he* was going to dress her. He meant the image consultants he'd hire, he corrected himself as she walked toward the front door.

He'd much rather *un*dress her.

No! That line of thinking was entirely inappropriate for tonight. This was a meeting. A business meeting to discuss important issues. He'd better not forget that fact for one minute while she was alone with him in the house.

He pushed open the storm door and grinned to hide his flustered state. "Hello! I'm glad you made it."

"Am I late?"

"No, not really. I was just hoping nothing had come up to keep you away. No problems."

"No, nothing. I dropped Jenny off at her friend's house and drove over."

"Great! Come on in." He held the door wide so she didn't have to brush against him as she passed inside. Unfortunately, that didn't keep her fragrance from wafting close. He inhaled deeply, breathing in her scent until he felt light-headed. Gripping the door tightly to keep from reaching out, he said a quick prayer for strength.

She turned around and frowned at him when she was halfway across the room. "Are you okay?"

"Sure. Why do you ask?" he asked as he peeled himself away from the storm door.

"Because you seem a little tense. Maybe a little hyper."

"Me? Hyper? No way. I'm fine."

She appeared skeptical, as she should be, but walked in and sat in a chair across from the couch. Good. He wouldn't be tempted to sit next to her. Slip his arms around her and pull her close so he could feel her curves and breathe in her scent.

He closed his eyes and clenched his fists. This was ridiculous. He was a thirty-two-year-old man, not a nineteen-year-old kid. He was supposed to have control over himself, but each time he was alone with Carole, he wanted her more and more.

"I'm glad you wanted to listen to my ideas," she said as she leaned back in the chair. Her skirt eased a little higher on her thighs, making Greg swallow and take a deep breath.

"Right. Would you like some iced tea?" He pushed a glass in her direction, not willing to risk accidentally touching her hand as he had when they'd first sat down for coffee and cookies at her house.

"Um...thanks." She tilted her head and frowned. "Are you sure you're okay?"

"I'm fine. Maybe a little nervous."

"Why?"

"Because I've been trying to get your cooperation ever since I came down here, and we really haven't been able to solve the problem."

"I don't want to get off on the wrong foot, but honestly, you've been trying to talk me into doing something I was very up-front about from the beginning. I simply don't want to be a spokesperson, a celebrity or anything else that would rob me of my privacy."

Greg shrugged. "I guess I have been a little overbearing, but like I've explained, my family's business is on the line.''

''I know, and that's why I'm here.''

Greg leaned closer and handed Carole a spoon. ''Is that the only reason you're here?'' He heard the intimate tone in his voice and immediately sat up straighter. ''Sorry. Forget I said that. I promised myself I wouldn't flirt, but I can't help myself.''

Carole sighed. ''I know. You're a natural flirt. A charmer. I saw you at the café, remember? You have all the women eating out of your hand.''

''All the women? What are you talking about?''

''My mother, Thelma. Even Jenny isn't immune to your charm. She thinks you're great, by the way. None of them will listen to me when I explain that you're a smooth talker who's after something.''

''Wait a minute! You make me sound like some sort of devious…Lothario. You're the only person I'm trying to talk into something. Something, I might add, that would be of great benefit to you.''

''Only if I'm motivated by money, which I'm not. Even if Huntington didn't pay me another penny for my cookie recipes, I'd survive. I'd get a real job, which wouldn't be as much fun as baking for a living. So I don't think that the carrot you're dangling is doing much good.''

''If you'll notice, I quit dangling that carrot a couple of days ago. I'm not talking about money being the benefit, although that's a big one, in my opinion. No, I'm talking about stretching yourself. Making yourself do something that isn't automatically comfortable so you'll learn and grow as a person.''

''I don't want to grow in that direction, thank-you-very-much.''

"Will you just tell me why? What terrible thing happened to make you so publicity shy?" He hadn't heard anything definite from Stewart Allen, except that Carole had no criminal background, bankruptcy, warrants or liens in any state. Greg was still waiting for more information on the personal stuff. Like whether she'd really been married, or if that was a story she or her family had created for the benefit of friends and family.

Carole added two spoons of sugar into her tea and stirred. Buying time. Greg recognized the move because he'd done it himself often enough when he needed to regroup.

She took a sip before answering. "I ran away and got married when I was only seventeen. I got pregnant with Jenny immediately, because I was stupid enough to believe that I couldn't get pregnant the first time I 'did it.' I wasn't mature enough to be a wife, much less a mother. Even so, she was going to be born. I never thought of any other option, even when she didn't seem real."

Greg nodded. After seeing Carole and Jennifer together, he also couldn't imagine life without the little girl.

"Fortunately, my mother came after me when she discovered where I'd run to. She brought me home and helped me end the marriage on the basis we were too young to make an adult decision."

"Did she know you were going to have a baby?"

Carole shook her head. "I didn't tell her until later. Not that I could hide it long. I swelled up like a blimp."

"I'll bet that's not true." He tried to imagine her rounded and ungainly, but the imagine wouldn't form in his mind. Still, he imagined she'd be beautiful, all glowing skin and motherly serenity. At least, that's how he thought pregnant women should look. He hadn't had much experience being around them yet, since his siblings were all single.

"Oh, it's true all right. Before running off, I used to strut around town in tight jeans and a big silver belt buckle from a regional pole-bending championship. I thought I was pretty hot stuff," she said with a chuckle. "I was so arrogant…and so stupid. I had no idea there was life beyond being an event champion or a rodeo queen. My thoughts and actions focused on looking good and expressing my independence."

"Until you had to suddenly grow up."

"Right. Suddenly people weren't talking about me because I'd won some event, gotten an award or just generally tried to be cute or clever. They started talking about me running off and coming home with my tail between my legs. About the tummy I couldn't hide beneath loose shirttails and unbuttoned jeans."

"The people of town seem really nice. I can't imagine that they were cruel." On the contrary, Thelma had been very protective of Carole. And everyone seemed to like Charlene Jacks, so he couldn't believe they would intentionally hurt her family.

"They weren't really cruel, but they weren't the only ones. You see, while I was gone, I was…involved with a band. There was a documentary shot that appeared on television. I was only a minor part of the story, but I really looked like a fool. A naive, stupid fool who fell for a complete jerk."

"Hey, lots of teens make mistakes."

She shook her head. "Not like me. I really messed up—not with drugs or anything, but just making bad decisions. Then I got my life straightened out, just in time for Jenny's birth. Once I had her, I promised myself and my family that I would never be in the position to be hurt by people—especially strangers—again. I would never put myself in the spotlight. My daughter would never suffer because of something I'd done to satisfy, indulge or enrich myself.''

Greg sighed. Her story was compelling. He had to face the fact that Carole might never change her mind. He couldn't think of one persuasive argument that she might listen to. She had a valid reason to be publicity shy, one he couldn't easily discount.

Maybe he shouldn't even try to tell her that her reasons were bogus. They were very real, very immediate to her.

''Okay, I understand now. And I want to thank you for telling me. Although I can't really imagine what happened when you ran off, or what being in that documentary was like, I can tell it was traumatic for you.''

''Yes, it was, but that's in the past. And that's where I want to keep it. I don't want my actions or things that happened to me brought up to Jenny. I don't want her to feel as though she was an unwanted by-product of my wild teenage years.''

''No, of course not.'' He was surprised to realize he felt so strongly that he didn't want anything ever to hurt the girl he'd grown to like very much. Not as a real daughter, he reminded himself. He was way too young, too career oriented, to have a ten-year-old.

Carole leaned back in her chair. ''So, now what?''

Chapter Eight

"Well, according to your contract, you've always been opposed to having someone else represent you to the public. Is that something we can discuss?"

She frowned, then said, "I suppose we can talk about it, but I can't imagine how we can agree on that, either. I don't want to deceive people with a fake Ms. Carole. Other companies have tried to hire actresses to portray their signature 'person,' real or imagined, but it usually doesn't work." She shuddered. "I definitely don't want to be turned into the equivalent of Ronald McDonald or Jack-in-the-box or even Betty Crocker."

Greg chuckled. "Do you remember when I told you that I'd imagined Aunt Bea or Alice of *The Brady Bunch?*"

"Please! No more clichés—television, advertising or otherwise."

"Okay. I promise I won't mention any of those characters to our advertising agency if you could work with us to find a suitable representative." Despite her teenage "mistake," Greg still believed the real Ms. Carole would be the most suitable person for the job. Unless, of course, Stewart Allen turned up something damaging. Huntington Foods couldn't survive another public relations fiasco without serious financial set-backs.

Not on my watch, he silently vowed.

"I still don't think it's necessary for the company—any company—to hire an actor or actress to portray someone for ads. I mean, what benefit could that possibly have for the consumer? Does a smiling woman holding a plate of cookies make the product look any better? Taste any better? I don't think so."

"I'll leave those questions to our advertising agency working with our internal publicity department. Right now, I'd like to know what *you* think are the most important traits for any 'Ms. Carole' to possess."

"Gosh, that's a tough question," she replied, reaching for her glass of iced tea.

Greg could just make out the shadow between her breasts, framed by the gap between the ties of her shirt. Peasant blouse, he remembered they were called. Carole certainly didn't look like any peasant he'd ever imagined. She looked classy and alluring and a dozen other complimentary adjectives.

"What do you think the product represents, then? I mean, why should someone buy our cookies? Or any cookies, for that matter?"

"Because they taste good? Isn't that enough?"

"Lots of things taste good." *Like you,* he wanted to add. His mouth went dry thinking about running his tongue alongside her neck until she shivered and arched against him.

"Cookies are an all-American tradition," she thoughtfully declared. "Made with ingredients that by themselves aren't great for you, but combined, satisfy us more than any other snack."

''Hmm. Satisfying. Wholesome. All-American. I think you're on a roll.'' All of those adjectives also applied to Carole, if she'd just realize it. Of course, he was most interested in the *satisfaction* part of her argument. ''Maybe I should start writing this down.'' And maybe he needed to cover the proof of his desire with a clipboard or at least a thick, yellow, lined tablet.

''When I think of cookies, I have to admit that a smiling mother, welcoming her child home from school or inviting her child's friends over for a snack comes to mind.'' She looked down at her hands and rubbed her thumb along her empty ring finger. ''After I had Jenny, I was still young. Just eighteen and already a mother. My mom helped me understand how to be a parent. Together, we were both parents. My sisters were great, too, especially Kerry, who was so supportive even though she worked and went to school. My younger sister, Cheryl, loved Jenny from the moment she was born and always offered to baby-sit to give me a little time for myself. I couldn't do much to repay them, so when I was alone at the house with the baby, I started baking. Since I always wanted things my way—that independent streak that got me into trouble to begin with—I decided I'd change the standard recipes for chocolate chip, sugar and several other cookie recipes to suit my own tastes. My sisters and mother were the recipients of my experiments.''

''I'll bet they enjoyed your efforts.''

Carole chuckled. ''Not all of them were so successful, but I remembered to write down the ones that were good. Pretty soon I was selling cookies to the Four Square Café and packaging them for sale at the Kash 'n' Karry and a couple of other businesses in the area.''

"You were an entrepreneur by the time you were what, nineteen?"

"About that," she answered, shrugging.

"How long did it take you to think about licensing the recipes?"

"Someone visiting town mentioned it as a way to make a living for myself and Jenny. She was almost three then."

Greg smiled. "So you were barely old enough to sign a contract when you negotiated with Huntington." He shook his head and chuckled. "And here I thought you were probably someone's grandmother."

Carole looked up and smiled. "Not quite. I hope I won't be a grandmother for a long time."

"Absolutely!" He didn't want to think about Jennifer having her own child anytime soon. Maybe when she was thirty or so. And Carole—why, she wouldn't look old enough to be a grandmother for at least twenty or thirty years.

He felt a sudden flash of panic. Was this what other men— fathers of adolescent girls, to be exact—experienced when they imagined their daughters dating? And why would he be thinking such a thing about Jennifer? He reminded himself *one more time* that he wasn't nearly old enough to be a father, so such thoughts were ridiculous.

"So, that's how I got in the cookie business and why I associate cookies with something positive. This whole controversy about how bad they are nutritionally...well, I just think it's silly. I mean, it's not as though cookies are the main source of food for anyone. Or anyone sensible."

"That's a very nice way of saying what my hotheaded brother was trying to express on national television.''

Carole chuckled. ''He didn't do such a very good job.''

''No, he didn't. Which is why I'm here, trying to talk you into doing something you really don't want to do.''

''That's right.''

''You really won't consider representing us? Because I have to tell you, you're the closest person to the wholesome, all-American, cookie-plate-holding mom that I could ever imagine.''

She smiled and shook her head. ''I'm sorry, Greg. I really am, because I understand your dilemma. And I understand how and why this is important to you. If I was heir to a big company like yours, one that had been in the family for years, I wouldn't want to see it hurt, either.''

Greg sighed, then stood. ''I suppose there's no reason to talk about it anymore then. Perhaps you can become a consultant for a possible Ms. Carole image to use for ads.''

''Well…perhaps,'' she replied, looking confused at his abrupt capitulation. ''I suppose I should go if we have nothing more to discuss.'' She stood, facing him across the table.

He walked around the coffee table. ''I just don't see how talking about the problem is going to make any difference.''

She nodded, looking a bit grim. Greg kept his features carefully blank, afraid he would suddenly grin. ''Will you be going back to Chicago…soon?''

He walked toward her. She appeared so petite and vulnerable as she stood in his living room. She wasn't really that tiny—probably five foot four or five inches in her bare feet, which he'd very much like to see. And she wasn't at all tiny in all the right places. Her curves had attracted him even before he'd become intrigued by her animated response to Jennifer in the arena. When he'd thought of her as *his* cowgirl.

"Soon, but I'll return," he replied, stopping close. Too close for her peace of mind, he knew.

"Why would—"

"Since we can't come to an agreement, and you won't become our spokesperson, there's no reason I can't do this," he said softly, reaching around, sliding his fingers to the hair at the nape of her neck. He pulled slightly, catching her off balance, as his mouth descended.

BEFORE SHE COULD take a breath, before she could move out of his way, his mouth descended on hers. Carole felt a moment of panic, an instant where she thought, *this is wrong. Then, this is so right.* This was no tentative exploration, but a full-blown kiss. An adult kiss.

The lightning struck. All ten zillion volts. She closed her eyes against the white-hot heat and absorbed the shock of his lips on hers, pressing, molding. His tongue stroked against the seam of her mouth and she opened to him. Oh, he was so patient, yet so insistent. He stroked, he overwhelmed. She felt both lightheaded and giddy, yet completely grounded and heavily sensual.

As his hands settled on her waist and pulled her close, as their bodies touched and rubbed and melted together, she felt something she'd never experienced before. Grown-up passion. Real, honest desire. Her hands wound higher, across his hard shoulders and around his neck.

But was this honest? Or was she deceiving herself? Was he deceiving her? She moaned as the questions rose, unbidden and unwelcome, throwing ice water on the passion she'd only just discovered. With a small cry of distress, she pushed against his chest.

"What's wrong?" he asked, his voice husky, his hands still on her waist.

"Why are we doing this?" She whispered, not knowing exactly what she meant, only reacting to her doubts.

"Because we've both wanted to for days. Because there's no reason we shouldn't."

"Because I said no to the business proposition?"

"That's right. I didn't want you to think I was trying to seduce you to get your compliance, not that I believed I could do any such thing. Not to you. But I knew we couldn't act on the attraction we both feel when the question of Huntington Foods was hanging between us." He pressed close, making her feel his desire, hot and hard against her belly. "I don't want anything between us."

"Oh, Greg, I…I can't believe this is best. That this is *real.*"

"Feels real to me," he said, tilting down until their foreheads touched, resting for a moment until she pulled away.

"I don't rush into relationships," she said shakily, turning and walking toward the side window. She ran her trembling fingers along the textured drapery fabric. "No, let me rephrase that. I haven't rushed into a relationship in over ten years."

"So, how slowly do you usually ease into a relationship," he asked, walking toward her, "just so I know what to expect? How patient do I need to be?" She felt panic grow as she anticipated his touch.

But he didn't press her. He stopped two feet away, appearing oh, so masculine and handsome, his blue-green eyes intense as he waited for her answer.

She took a deep breath, trying to compose herself. "I don't know. I've *never* eased into a relationship. I know this sounds completely pitiful, but I don't do relationships. Ever."

"Never?"

"Never ever," she answered, smiling slightly.

A moment of something…maybe fear, appeared in his eyes. But why would he be afraid of what she said? Or maybe he was just appalled. He was accustomed to women who were modern and sophisticated, not old-fashioned and countrified. Not women who simply didn't have affairs.

"Oh," he finally said, looking confused but no less desirable. At least to her unsophisticated eyes.

She shrugged, then let her hands fall to her side. "But I can't deny that I'm attracted to you. I was afraid for you to kiss me, but I wanted you to just the same."

"I know. I know all that, and I know that the attraction, the passion we feel is real. I want you, Carole, and I think we'd be darned good together."

"But for how long? For a day, three days? You're not staying in Ranger Springs. You have no reason to stay, now that I've said no to your proposal." She felt a rush of heat at her word choice. "I mean, your business plan."

He smiled. "I know what you meant, and you're

right. I'm not staying in Ranger Springs for long. But we still have unfinished business.''

''What?''

''I think you could be a darn good consultant to find someone to represent the company. I still need your help.''

''You do?''

''Yes.'' He stepped closer. ''Except, now, because you won't become our spokesperson, you won't think I'm trying to influence you by...well, through this attraction we feel. What you said earlier about what cookies mean, about what the company should stand for, was very true and insightful. Huntington could still use your help, only, this time it won't be personal. We won't ask you to do something you don't want to do. So you see? Our business isn't finished. Not yet.''

She put a hand against his chest to keep him away, but his heat and well-toned muscles distracted her from her thoughts. ''What...what are you going to do about this personal thing?''

''I'm going to try my best to convince you that we should be together. Like you said, not because we're both interested in forever, but because we can't ignore this feeling. And I'm going to ask for your help in saving my company through finding someone perfect to represent us to the public.''

''I...I suppose I could do that.''

He smiled as his hand covered hers. ''I'm counting on it.''

She pulled away once more, skirting around the chair, heading toward the front door. ''I meant the part about finding a representative.''

He smiled, appearing male and predatory even

though he stood still beside the window. "I meant all of it."

"I need time," she said weakly, "about the other part."

He nodded. "I can give you four or five days. I have to get back to Chicago for some meetings, but I'll return by the weekend. Monday at the latest."

"What about the place you're renting? What about your steer?"

"I'm sure Jennifer would love to spend more time with him before she leaves for camp."

"Are you saying you expect us to pet-sit your steer?"

"I'm asking you to please take care of him for a few days."

Carole took a deep breath. "Are you sure you're coming back?"

"You can count on it." He smiled, appearing very dangerous to her peace of mind. "As a matter of fact, you couldn't keep me away now that you've given me a taste of what's to come."

"We have a saying here. 'Don't count your chickens before they hatch.'"

"I have a saying, too. A motto, really. Never Give Up." He pushed away from the window and took a step toward her. "Never Give Up," he repeated, his tone low and intimate.

She fled for the front door before she gave him another taste...and maybe even the whole meal.

CAROLE KNEW that Puff was to stay with them for at least three or four days—maybe more, if Greg was in Chicago longer than anticipated. He'd put feed and hay into her stock trailer when they'd moved the steer, as she'd stood back and watched his muscles flex beneath his T-shirt, lusting after him as she'd never desired another man.

Now she stood on her front porch and waved as he drove away in his rental car. She had a reprieve, just as Jenny's steer had gotten a stay of execution thanks to Greg's generous bid at the arena. The action that had brought him to Ranger Springs had far-reaching consequences, from saving steers to inspiring lust in a previously sensible, circumspect mother of a ten-year-old.

Okay, maybe she wasn't over the hill, as she sometimes tried to pretend so she didn't seem so out of touch with other young women her age. Many of them weren't married, or, if they were, didn't have children yet. She was the exception: a healthy twenty-eight-year-old whose only previous sexual experience had been with a nineteen-year-old boy who she'd insisted should marry her first. And the extent of that experience had lasted all of two months, over ten years ago.

How in the world could she even consider making love with Greg Rafferty? Despite the attraction they felt, she would be so rusty in the bedroom that he'd probably laugh all the way back to Chicago. Or get that kind look in his eyes that said, "That's okay. You tried."

She hugged her arms around herself and shuddered despite the ninetysomething-degree heat. She was insane to think about getting naked with a man she'd known for less than a week. Absolutely insane.

But, oh, she wanted him. She really, really wanted to know what making love with Greg Rafferty would feel like.

"Mom! Look at Puff! He remembers where I keep

the grain bucket.'' Jenny's excited chatter from the direction of the barn brought Carole back to reality faster than a splash of cold water.

"I'll be right there, sweetie,'' she replied as she glanced once more at the driveway. Not even a faint cloud of dust remained from where Greg had driven off. Maybe she should remember that image when she considered what to do about her long-dormant love life. Did she really want indelible memories of a man who would vanish from her life like a wisp of smoke?

GREG SETTLED into the leather seat of the modest but comfortable jet his family used for Huntington business. Roberta Huntington Rafferty had developed a fear of flying the major carriers when a good friend had died in a commercial airline crash, so the board of directors had approved the luxury. Greg often thanked his mother for her phobia because the company jet meant no delays due to shuffling aircraft or crews, no body searches at check-in, and no conforming to airline schedules.

He used his cell phone to call the office. Within a few minutes he'd scheduled appointments with his father, mother and sister to discuss Carole's outright refusal to become Huntington's spokesperson. He also wanted to present his alternative plan: have her become so involved in finding a suitable person that she soon realized *she* really was the perfect woman for the job.

This was a gamble, but he had few options. In the meantime, Huntington's PR department was working fast and furious with the ad agency to develop new commercials that stressed the old, family business, their commitment to excellence and their goal of providing snacks enjoyed by children and parents alike. The board had briefly suggested *he* star in the commercials, putting a real face and name up there for people to focus on. However, Greg felt that because he was Brad's brother—they even closely resembled each other—that solution wasn't a good one.

These were all stop-gap measures, anyway, designed to reinforce the previous goodwill of the public for Huntington. But they needed a major overhaul, one that focused on one person, one message, for the long haul. He still couldn't believe how perfect Carole was for the position. She had everything: good looks, personality, small-town roots and credibility.

"Five minutes to takeoff, Mr. Rafferty," the pilot said over the intercom system. Greg fastened his seat belt and hoped for good weather between the Hill Country and the Windy City. His brother, Brad, had caused enough "bumpy rides" to last a lifetime.

Greg still needed to know what exactly constituted an "unfortunate incident" in the eyes of her friends and neighbors. How personal was the problem? He knew whatever had happened wasn't a legal issue. Now he needed to discover whether it was a moral one—one that the public might find objectionable.

He wouldn't think less of Carole if she hadn't actually married Jennifer's father. So perhaps she'd told people she'd been married because she didn't want her daughter to have a stigma. After all these years she couldn't change her story. Or maybe she had been married. Perhaps the young man who'd fathered Jennifer was now an embarrassment. He could be a deadbeat or worse. That documentary she'd mentioned could have been on an embarrassing topic, perhaps something illegal or immoral that he'd done.

Certainly no one in town wanted to talk about him. Which made him believe Jennifer's father, not Carole or her decision, might be the problem.

He looked out the window as they started to taxi, the engines whining with restrained power. Outside, the hot Texas landscape rolled by like an old, silent movie, the film sepia in color. He'd like to see this place in spring or fall. Maybe, if he could establish a working relationship with Carole, he could come back periodically. Perhaps they could conduct a discreet affair. Something that wouldn't harm anyone: Jennifer, Carole or her family.

Greg found it increasingly difficult to separate Carole's potential with Huntington from his personal feelings for her. Hell, even if she had some huge embarrassment in her past, he knew that wouldn't stop him from wanting her. She seemed perfect for both roles—spokesperson and lover—if she wasn't harboring some terrible secret.

Except she didn't want to be the spokesperson and she probably didn't want to become his lover. She was a forever kind of woman. She didn't have affairs. She didn't jump into bed with men who were going to be in town temporarily. He belonged in Chicago, where the family business was headquartered. Where he'd trained and planned to take over that corner office for nearly as long as he could remember.

No matter how appealing he found Carole and her daughter, how friendly the town, how cute the steer seemed—when he wasn't being a royal pain in the...blisters—they weren't worth giving up his dream. He was the C.E.O. of his family business, responsible for turning around the public perception of Huntington Foods.

The jet lifted into the air, taking him far away from Ranger Springs. He knew, however, that Carole Jacks wouldn't be far from his thoughts.

Chapter Nine

Carole stuffed an extra granola bar, a tissue and a tube of lip balm into Jenny's bright-pink backpack. "Are you sure you have everything? We could go over it one more time."

"Mom, it's all packed. I checked off the list, see?" She held up the sheet the camp provided, and sure enough, little checkmarks in glittery purple ink were placed beside each item. Jenny had insisted on packing herself this year.

One more indication that her little girl was growing up. Before long she'd be wearing a bra and talking to boys on the telephone.

Carole held back a shudder at the thought as they walked through the front door. Soon she wouldn't have a little girl any longer. She'd always be Jenny's mother, but little by little, she was needed less and less. Not that she defined herself by her role as "Mom," but still, she loved being a mother. She would have loved to have given Jenny a little brother or sister…but not enough to get involved with a man she didn't love.

Which immediately made her think of Greg. She didn't love him, of course, but she did lust after him.

She'd thought about him day and night since he left on Wednesday. And she thought about *them*. If there could be a *them*, at least temporarily.

She wasn't sure if she had the nerve to go through with an affair. Just the word made her cringe. She didn't do affairs. She'd never had casual sex. After ten years, she could barely remember having sex, period. And what she did remember wasn't all that great. Kind of exciting, in a rushed, sweaty, messy way.

Somehow she imagined Greg wouldn't be nearly as quick, sweaty or messy as Johnny Ray. Not that she was expecting the kind of fireworks and musical crescendos as in movies and books. She figured the intensity of feeling increased with the dramatic license of the director or author.

All she knew was that when Greg kissed her, she wanted to mold her body to his, feel his skin and taste him all over. That had never happened before.

"Mom!"

Carole shook herself out of her inappropriate thoughts. "What, sweetie?"

"I asked if you would take Puff for a walk at least once a day. You know he likes to eat those weeds out at the end of the driveway."

Carole smiled, hoping she didn't look flushed. "Of course. I'll make sure he doesn't forget how to lead."

"And when Mr. Rafferty gets back from Chicago, maybe he could come over and see Puff, too. I think Puff likes him."

Yeah, I like him, too. "I'm sure he'll want to come by and see Puff. Remember, Mr. Rafferty does own him."

"I know, but I don't think he wants him for real."

No, but I want Greg Rafferty, Carole acknowledged.

"When the feed runs out and we have to cut back your allowance to buy more, you'll wish Mr. Rafferty were still taking care of that big hay burner."

"Oh, Mom."

Carole heard a vehicle and looked out, expecting to see Megan's mother. She was driving the girls to camp, which was north, near Glen Rose. Instead, she spotted a familiar luxury sedan. The windows were tinted, but she knew he was driving. Her heartbeat began to race and her palms grew damp.

"Is that Mr. Rafferty?" Jenny asked.

"I do believe…I think it is," Carole replied, sounding a bit breathless. She hoped her curious daughter didn't ask why her normally sensible mother suddenly couldn't speak like a responsible adult.

"Neat! I'm glad he came back before I left."

Me, too! Carole nearly blurted out. She grasped her hands tightly, feeling the pressure. She had to make a decision soon about them. But for now, all she could think about was *He was here. He was here!*

Greg pulled to a stop near the porch. A moment later the driver's side door opened and he stepped out, smiling as he shielded his eyes against the noonday sun. The man needed sunglasses if he wasn't going to wear a hat.

Today he'd dressed in a body-hugging sea-green polo shirt that hugged his wide chest. He'd tucked it into light khaki chinos, and on his feet, instead of the blister-producing ropers, he wore casual deck shoes and no socks.

He appeared very preppy, which was probably closer to the "real" Greg Rafferty than the catalog cowboy.

"You came back," she said unnecessarily, her

voice again sounding a little breathless. A little young and insecure. "Early," she added, deepening her tone. "You came back earlier than I expected."

"I didn't want to miss seeing Jennifer before she went off to camp," Greg said easily, walking to the front porch, ruffling her daughter's hair as he bestowed a big grin.

"Thank you," Jenny replied, her tone happy as she spontaneously hugged Greg. "It was fun having Puff home again."

"I keep telling your mother than can be arranged permanently."

"Mom!"

"Oh, look," Carole exclaimed, pointing at the road where Megan's mother's van was pulling into the driveway. "Your ride is here."

"We'll talk about this later, young lady," Jenny mimicked. She sounded so silly, trying to be both funny and grown-up, that Carole had to laugh.

"I'll get your duffel. You can say goodbye to Mr. Rafferty." Carole escaped to the cooler interior of the house where Jenny's camping gear, clothes, towels and other assorted necessities lay packed on the entry floor. Her daughter's life, neatly rolled and stuffed into one canvas bag.

Oh, she was going to miss her baby.

When she went back outside, Greg had a hand on Jenny's shoulder and both were smiling. The sight gave her pause, because Jenny didn't usually take to strangers that easily. She seemed to genuinely like Greg, which could be a problem when he no longer came to see them. Carole had to admit he was good with her daughter, though. Greg had shown an abundance of both patience and perseverance in the past week.

Had it been only a week and one day since he'd charged into their lives? She felt as though she'd known him much longer.

Megan and Ashley piled out of the van as Jenny ran over, each excited about the annual trip. The girls loved staying in the cabins, swimming in the small lake and riding horses. They learned new skills every summer, from campfire cooking to archery to water rescue.

Carole had often wished she could go with them, but moms weren't invited. And children needed time away, she reminded herself, so they could grow independent and self-confident. No matter how hard it was on parents.

Carole wanted to provide a good example for her daughter. Sometimes the responsibility seemed overwhelming because she was a single parent. That's one of the reasons she wouldn't consider becoming Greg's company spokesperson; she needed to be home for Jenny to savor every moment of her daughter's childhood. Greg just didn't understand how important that duty was to a single mother.

Within minutes the duffel and backpack were loaded in the back of the van, and then it was time for hugs. And no tears. Carole put on her brave "mom" face and told Jenny what a great time she'd have.

"I'll miss you, Mommy," accompanied by one of Jenny's big hugs, nearly sent Carole over the edge.

"I'll miss you, too," she replied, holding on a second or two longer. "I'll see you on Saturday, okay?"

Jenny nodded, then pulled away, smiling, and jumped into the van.

So much for lingering goodbyes. Every year they got a little shorter.

Carole waved, then crossed her arms over her chest and hugged herself. What was she going to do when Jenny went off to college in eight short years? She'd only be thirty-six years old—an age at which a lot of career women were just starting their families.

The van pulled out slowly onto the highway, then picked up speed as they headed north. Carole watched until it was out of sight, swallowed up by the bend in the road and the mesquite grove at the edge of her property.

"Well, that's that," she said, mostly to herself.

"You miss her already," Greg commented, standing beside her, looking in the same direction as the departing van.

"Every year," she said, sniffing just a little. "I miss her giggles and her silly music, her complaints about chores and her pleas to spend the night with friends. But she'll be back before I know it, full of stories about the other campers and the counselors and all the animals she saw in the wilds."

"I could keep you company," Greg offered casually.

"Don't you have a business to run?"

"I'm partially on vacation this week."

"How can you go partially on vacation? Doesn't that negate the effect of getting away from work, which is what vacation is all about?"

"Not when the working part of my vacation is *you,*" he replied, turning toward her, drawing her hands away and looping them around his neck, then lowering his head for a kiss.

GREG COULDN'T CONVINCE Carole to get out of her house. She insisted she wanted to be alone. He didn't like the thought of her moping around, thinking of her absent daughter. Carole needed to "get a life" that didn't involve family, cookies or motherhood, but he knew he couldn't convince her of that fact. She was a grown woman. A gorgeous, intelligent, *stubborn* woman.

He drove to his rented house and unloaded his suitcase. Feeling a little hot and restless from his flight, he decided on a swim. And after swimming laps until he was pleasantly tired and lying in the sun for all of ten minutes, he realized he was still restless. Still hot.

The day was too quiet. There was no twelve-hundred-pound "baby" bawling in the pasture for extra food or attention. He didn't expect any visitors; he didn't have any unfinished stack of paperwork that needed his attention. Such idleness wasn't in his nature; at least, not in the past twelve years or so.

"Damn." Was this how Carole felt, rattling around her empty house? He'd never felt quite as alone before, knowing Carole was just a few miles away but oh, so untouchable.

At least for now.

He had to give her time if she was really emotionally distraught over Jennifer going to camp, although he couldn't really understand her feelings. Even if she wasn't upset, he had to respect her wishes to be alone, since he had no right to impose his opinions or values on her. Although he wanted her fiercely for personal reasons and needed her desperately for business purposes, they weren't even friends. They didn't know each other that well. If not for the strong attraction they both felt, he wouldn't have returned to Ranger

Springs. He'd be back in Chicago, looking at publicity photos of aspiring spokespersons. Coming up with Plan B that he could present to the board.

Instead, he was trying to understand a woman unlike any other he'd ever known. His own mother certainly hadn't spent precious hours grieving about her children going away for a week or two. He'd always known that his parents used his and his siblings' absences as an opportunity to get more of their own agenda accomplished. They might host a business meeting, take a short trip or attend cultural events with important customers or suppliers.

On several occasions during the first days he'd been in Ranger Springs, he'd noticed Carole looking wistfully at Jennifer, as though she was concerned over her daughter's future. Or perhaps her opportunities. Maybe Carole was just a worrier, but he didn't think so. Something about her daughter made her edgy, and he didn't know what.

He also didn't know her well enough to ask, but he probably would, very soon. After all, getting to know her better was the main reason he'd come back to Texas. If he could also get her to agree to be Huntington's spokesperson, well, that would be an added bonus.

He stretched on the chaise lounge by the pool, thinking of going inside for a snack, when he heard gravel crunch on the driveway. He couldn't see anything due to the privacy fence surrounding the pool, so he listened. Sure enough, there was a car…or maybe a pickup truck…stopping in front of his house.

Since he wasn't expecting visitors, he could think of only one person who might be looking for him.

With a smile he pushed himself up, grabbed a towel to sling around his neck and jogged toward the patio door.

CAROLE COUNTED TO FIVE before she rang the door-bell, telling her heart to return to a normal beat, asking her lungs to provide enough air so she didn't look as though she'd run all the way from her house to his. But she obviously wasn't very good at controlling her reactions, at least to Greg Rafferty, because she felt just as nervous now as when she'd decided to drive over.

He flung open the door, a big smile on his face, giving him a boyish charm. Then she looked lower and all thoughts of "boys" left her brain. He was wearing those practically nonexistent swim trunks again.

He looked really, really good in them.

"Hello, Carole. Come on in," he said, holding open the storm door.

She tried to smile in return, but expected her efforts weren't successful. He didn't seem to mind her lack of response, continuing to smile at her. She eased by his damp body, smelling both cologne and chlorinated water as she came so close to all that bare skin.

"Can I get you something to drink? I'm not sure what I have in the—"

"No, that's okay," she said, walking briskly into the living room. She turned around, her mouth dry as she watched him close the door. Oh, Lord. His backside was perfect. Broad shoulders with just the right mix of muscle and bone, a long, furrowed spine that disappeared into the waist of his Speedo. An absolutely fantastic butt, with just enough muscle and curve to make her want to hold on tight.

"Maybe some water," she said, again breathless as he walked across the small entryway toward her.

"Okay. Make yourself comfortable. I'll be back in a flash."

She eased onto the couch, then changed her mind and sat in the overstuffed chair beside the fireplace. No, this wasn't right, either. What was she, Goldilocks? She dragged the rocking chair closer to the couch and end table and sat down. Ah, much better. She could be comfortable here. Or as comfortable as possible given what she had to say.

She'd never done anything like this before. Edgy enough to pace the room, she made herself stay seated, but rocked until she thought she might rub grooves into the floor. What was taking him so long? Didn't he realize she had something important to say?

"Here you go," Greg said, returning from the kitchen with two glasses.

"Thank you." Her gaze automatically went to his…swimwear as he stood beside her chair. He'd covered himself in running shorts and a soft-as-sin T-shirt. So much for stealing glances at what she'd been missing for ten years.

"I'm glad to see you, but rather surprised. I thought you wanted to be alone."

"I did. I needed to think. You know how sometimes you just need time?"

"I think so," he answered as he took a seat on the couch, placing his water next to hers on the end table.

"So, Jenny is off to camp, and now you're back in town, and I wasn't real sure what I wanted to do about that."

"You mean other than ask me to leave you alone again?"

She frowned at him. "If I didn't want to see you, I would have stayed home."

"Good point. So, back to my original question. Why are you here?"

She started rocking. Then she realized how restless she must look, so she stopped. And sighed. "I...I've been thinking."

"About our unfinished business?" he asked, leaning forward, his hands clasped between his widespread knees.

"Well...yes."

"Personal business?" he asked, his voice low and husky. Sexy.

She nodded.

"And you made a decision?"

"I think so."

"That's not very decisive, Ms. Carole," he said, rising from the couch.

As she watched him, her heart began to race and her palms grew damp. She wasn't ready for this. She'd made a mistake. This was too much, too soon. But he didn't seem to understand all that as he reached down, took her hands and lifted her from the rocking chair.

She felt surprised that her legs supported her.

"Did you come here to tell me you've decided that we should become lovers?"

"That sounds kind of..."

"Decisive?" he supplied, pulling her closer.

She closed her eyes as their bodies brushed together. "I told you I'm not good at this."

"No, you told me you don't *do* this. That doesn't mean you're not good at it."

"If I'm this nervous just trying to talk to you, I can't imagine that I'll be able to do anything else, no matter what I convinced myself when I was alone at the house.''

His hands stroked her arms, then settled on her back, pulling her tighter. ''We're going to be fine. Just try to relax.''

''Relax!'' She tried to chuckle. ''I feel like one big, exposed nerve.''

''Yeah?'' he said softly, smiling. ''That's good.''

''It is?'' She didn't think what she was feeling was good. Or even normal. ''I don't think so. I think this is what happens when a normal, healthy woman goes too long without…you know.''

''Sex?'' he asked, smiling casually even as his eyes burned hot and intense.

She nodded. ''Honestly, Greg, I don't think this is going to work. Maybe I need more time.''

''Maybe you need to be kissed.''

''I just don't—''

''Hush,'' he whispered, pulling her tight against his body. Then his lips came down on hers. She shut her eyes, overwhelmed by sensation. Firm lips, a very insistent tongue, a warm, solid chest. And lower, the evidence of his desire, pressing hot and hard against her belly.

His lips molded to hers, slanting, commanding a response. She moaned, which seemed to inflame him, although he didn't lose control. No, he just became more demanding of a response, so she complied, rubbing against him, meeting his tongue, thrust for thrust.

Oh, heavens. His mouth left hers and traced a path to her jaw, her neck. It had been too long. She felt…she wasn't sure what she felt. She wanted to crawl inside his body. She wanted to rip off his T-shirt and run her hands all over his smooth, hot skin.

She wanted to run her tongue all over him. She wished he were still wet from a swim, nearly naked in his Speedo.

She'd never wanted to lick a man dry before.

Her hands fisted in the worn cotton of his shirt, pulling it up, up from his shorts. Her fingers itched to touch him, but she held back. She didn't know what he liked, what he expected. And her head was spinning, her heart pounding heavily in her chest.

"Touch me," he whispered against her neck, his breath ragged and hot.

Had he read her mind? Or had she spoken aloud? She wasn't sure. But he'd given her permission to do exactly what she wanted. How could she resist?

Her hands unclenched from his T-shirt, then slowly moved beneath the hem to touch his back. His skin was hot, smooth, stretched tight. She moved upward, to his shoulderblades, then sank her fingers into the strong muscles she discovered there.

He moaned.

"I'm sorry."

"No, that was a good moan. Your hands feel wonderful on me. You feel good all over. I'm just wondering if you're getting a little warm. Like maybe we're overdressed?"

Getting naked. That's what he was talking about. She'd thought about that aspect of having an affair, but couldn't quite conjure up the image of removing her clothes in broad daylight in front of a man she'd known a week. No, she didn't have that good an imagination.

"I'm fine the way I am right now," she said, trying to keep her voice even, "but you go ahead if you're too hot."

Greg chuckled, then started laughing. Before she knew what he'd planned, he lifted her off her feet, their bodies even more perfectly aligned. My, he was tall. And strong. She resisted the urge to wrap her legs around his waist and hold on tight.

"If this is going to work, you're going to have to relax."

"I can't relax," she confessed, burying her face in his neck. "Everything you do or suggest makes me feel like I'm going to jump out of my skin."

"That's because *I'm* doing things to *you.*"

"What do you mean?" she asked, looking up as he carried her down the hallway toward the bedrooms.

"I mean, you need to get more involved. If you're not busy, you'll start thinking again."

"So you want a brainless lover?"

"No, I want someone who's involved *with* me. Who makes me feel as if she wants me as much as I want her."

"I do want you," she whispered against his neck.

He stopped, pressed her against the wall next to the bedroom door and kissed her until her head swam. Her arms tightened around his neck as her legs framed his arousal. She'd never been so sexually aware before. Every move, every breath, increased her excitement.

He broke the kiss and carried her into the bedroom. At least it was somewhat darker in here…just in case he looked at her naked. Which she still wasn't sure she wanted him to do. Slipping unobserved between the sheets would be so much easier, but somehow she didn't think Greg would allow her to be modest.

She'd bounced back to her prepregnancy weight pretty well after Jennifer had been born, but she had the stretch marks to prove she'd given birth to an eight-pound baby. Greg Rafferty probably wasn't used to women with stretch marks. He didn't seem like the type who dated women with kids. And women in his dating circle who had given birth probably had their stretch marks removed with lasers or some other modern technology.

"Maybe we should talk about this first," she hedged.

"I talk better lying down."

"I doubt that. You never had any trouble talking before, sitting up."

"Try me and see." He carried her across the room to the queen-size bed.

She took a deep breath. "If I say stop, we stop."

"Of course. I want you, but I'm not some animal who can't restrain himself."

No, she seemed to be the only one out of control. Right now, with the backs of her legs touching the mattress, she felt as though she might start shaking any moment. Especially when he slowly eased her down his body, still holding on tight. She doubted her legs would support her.

"If we have an affair," she said, drawing in a deep breath, "it's only for as long as you're in town. I don't want you to think I'll try to contact you in Chicago or show up at your condo, making a scene."

"Whatever you want. I have no problem with continuing a relationship even after I go back home."

"I don't think that would work because another requirement is that you don't sleep with anyone else while you and I are involved."

"No problem. And I would say I expect the same, but I know you wouldn't do that anyway."

So now she felt like a heel for implying he had no morals. *Great start to the affair, Carole.*

"Thank you, and I didn't mean to imply you would do something like that. I just wanted you to understand some of the rules I've been thinking of."

"I don't believe we need many rules, Carole. This is about two people who want each other. I certainly don't want to hurt you, Jennifer or your family. As long as we're discreet, I don't see the problem."

The problem is that I might do something really stupid like fall in love with you if I'm not careful. "I think it's good to talk."

"Talking can be good, but I think we've said everything that needs to be said. I think we're both ready for some action."

Chapter Ten

Action. Such a simple word, but she had no idea where to start. Okay, she had an idea. She'd like to get a closer look at his incredible body and touch his warm, smooth skin. She'd like for him to kiss her again, hold her close and assure her she was wonderful. That she was doing great.

"First, we are wearing way too many clothes."

"Right. You first," she suggested.

He chuckled. "You aren't that shy, are you?"

"I'm pretty shy."

"Then let's compromise. I take something off, you take something off. Deal?"

"O-okay." *I can do this,* she told herself. She didn't look bad. And it was kind of dark in the bedroom, even though it was broad daylight outside. She and Johnny Ray had made love in the daylight. A long, long time ago.

At least Greg wasn't throwing her down on the bed and rushing her with sloppy kisses and pawing hands. Not that he'd do any such thing.

He whipped his T-shirt over his head and grinned.

She pulled apart the snaps on her shirt, each "pop" loud in the silence of the bedroom as she watched the fabric separate. When she got to the last one, she looked up at Greg.

"Next time I get to do the shirt," he said in a husky voice, his breathing rapid. "I never knew how sexy those shirts could be, although I have to confess to some pretty vivid fantasies during the past week."

His words made her smile, easing just a little of her nervousness. She longed to run her hands down his heaving chest, across his defined ribs, but she didn't. Not when she was shrugging out of her shirt and letting him see her new baby-blue, lacy underwire bra that gave herself just a little more cleavage.

She just couldn't make herself buy black or red, which were probably sexier. She'd decided to start with the pastels and work up to bolder colors…if the affair lasted that long.

"I'm not sure this is going to work."

Her gaze snapped back to his face. Had she already done something wrong? "Why?"

"Because you have on way more clothes than me. I'm going to be buck naked while you're still dressed in that sexy underwear. Not a good idea in my current condition. Let's revise the rules. You take off two pieces of clothing for each one of mine."

"I'm not sure I like you changing the rules in the middle of things."

"We're not in the middle yet. We've just started." He ran his hands down her bare arms, making her shiver. "Trust me."

She took a deep breath, which made his eyes widen as he stared at her…bra. She hadn't planned to swell her chest so much, but he obviously appreciated it. She'd have to try that again. Later. When she felt more brave. For now, she had more undressing to do.

"Do shoes count?"

"Not for you, since I'm not wearing any."

She gave herself more time by easing off her tennis shoes and kicking them out of the way. Too bad they didn't count; there were two of them.

Okay, moment of truth, she thought as she tackled the buttons on her jeans. If he was going to be turned off by her stretch marks, she'd know soon enough. She glanced at the impressive bulge in his shorts. No, not turned off yet.

The blue lace of her panties barely showed when she started shimmying out of the denim. She had to lean back against the mattress to take them the rest of the way off. Finally she kicked the jeans away and stood up straight.

"I'm feeling a little awkward here," she said nervously as he continued to look. She shrugged and let her hands fall to her sides.

"I'm feeling a little awkward myself. You haven't done this in ten years? I feel as if I haven't, either. In fact, I'm feeling a bit like a teenager myself. I hope I have better control now than I did when I was eighteen."

Lord, she hoped so, too. She didn't recall control being one of Johnny Ray's greatest assets, not that she could even compare the two men. Her husband had been a boy; Greg was a man. A very *large* man.

"Your turn," she said, hot and flushed. She wished he'd turned on the ceiling fan. Maybe then she wouldn't feel as if she was about to boil over, especially when his hands went to the waist of his shorts and eased them lower.

The elastic caught on his erection, barely contained by white briefs. She sucked in a breath, imagining the feel of fabric against his aroused flesh. She wanted to ''help'' him by kneeling down, removing the shorts inch by inch. She wanted to do a lot of things she'd never done before.

Her legs started trembling and her mouth felt as dry as the Texas plains in July. Time seemed suspended. Was he never going to finish undressing?

''Is it hot in here?'' she asked rhetorically. Greg just smiled and continued to slowly remove his shorts.

She spun away, unable to watch. Spotting the wall switch to the ceiling fan, she turned it on, praying the setting was on high. She needed help so she didn't burst into flames. Fortunately the attached lights weren't turned on, so she was saved more intense scrutiny. Cool air swept her body as she turned back to Greg.

''Your turn,'' he announced, hands on his lean hips.

''Would you like to lie down and talk some more?''

''Nope.''

Carole sighed, then walked over to the spot where she'd undressed before. Closer to Greg. Closer to that bed. Her shaking hands went to the rear clasp of her bra and fumbled. And fumbled.

''Need some help?''

''No!'' She groaned in frustration. She'd done this a zillion times. Why couldn't she do it now? ''Yes.''

He stepped around her, flicking open the catch as though he'd performed the task a zillion times. Maybe he had. To other women. Other lovers.

Don't think about that now. Just get on with it, while he's behind you and maybe not looking so intently at your body. Right. She could practically feel laser beams scanning her from breasts to legs and back up again.

He eased the straps off her shoulders, and her new bra fell to the ground. Her nipples contracted almost painfully in the cool breeze from the fan.

Okay, just get it over with. She grabbed the elastic of her matching blue-lace panties and skimmed them down her legs as quickly as possible, realizing too late that her butt was sticking out, bare naked. She jerked upright, face flaming, and kicked the panties in the direction of her jeans. Why couldn't she be one of those women who undressed seductively? She'd seen them in movies and Victoria's Secret television ads.

"Carole?" His whisper came from beside her, by her right shoulder.

"Yes?"

"Open your eyes and look at me."

She hadn't realized she'd closed her eyes. She hadn't even realized where he was, but knew he still watched her. She felt his gaze like sunshine on a cloudless day, burning her skin wherever it touched. She wondered if she'd show burns tomorrow from her exposure to Greg. She turned around.

He slowly took in her body, from her messy hair to her level shoulders to her nice-size, but not quite "pert" breasts, to her faintly stretch-marked belly and lower. Okay, now he knew she was a natural blond.

"It's a sin to hide that body under clothes."

Her attention snapped to his face. Was he serious?

She thought he was reaching for her, but instead, he yanked back the bedspread and top sheet in one sudden movement. The scent of fresh linen filled the air.

Then his hands came to rest on her waist, his thumbs just inches from her breasts. "You are so beautiful you take my breath away."

"I'm not—"

"You are. I'm in awe. I think perhaps we should lie down now, but not to talk. Are you okay with that?" He sounded husky and shaky and oh, so sexy.

She was more than okay; she was melting into a puddle on the carpet. She nodded, not trusting her voice. With a quick lift he deposited her on the mattress. She had the ridiculous urge to ask him which side he preferred, which almost made her giggle. Nervous energy, she realized. She scooted into the middle of the mattress and watched.

Instead of immediately joining her, he quickly removed those white briefs—his last article of clothing. The only thing that kept her from seeing all of him. She felt her eyes widen. Oh, my.

He smiled as he placed a knee on the mattress and slid toward her. "Don't worry. We'll take it slow."

Slow? She wanted it fast. She wanted it now. She wanted all those fantasies she'd experienced only in her mind, and especially in the last week.

Her legs shifted restlessly on the bed as he eased down beside her. "You don't have to treat me like I'm going to break. I'm a strong woman."

"I know you are, but lifting feed sacks and taking care of your land and house are different from making love. Especially when you haven't done it in a long time."

"I've had a baby. I don't know how that…changes things."

"Don't worry about it," he said, leaning down to place a kiss on the upper slope of her breast. "You'll find out soon enough how well we fit."

"Kiss me, Greg," she whispered, sliding her hands around his back, pulling him close. The feel of his bare chest against her made her gasp. She arched off the bed to be closer. Closer.

His lips sealed tightly over hers, pressing her down, making her moan. His hands sculpted her body as his tongue thrust inside her mouth, mimicking the motion of her hips. She wanted everything *right now.* She felt as though she'd burst into flames if she didn't get it *right now.*

His leg eased between her restless ones, his thigh pressing against her there. *Yes, there,* she wanted to cry out. She felt his arousal against her leg and wanted to touch him, but she didn't want to let go of him. What he was doing felt so good. He felt so good beneath her grasping fingers. Was she holding him too tight? Making a mark with her short fingernails? She didn't know, and as he pressed his leg higher against her, she didn't care.

He reached down and captured her nipple, rolling it between his fingers so expertly she broke away from the kiss and gasped. The feeling was so near pain she wanted to cry out, but such incredible pleasure that she arched higher, offering him everything.

More, she wanted to shout, and then he bent his head and took her other nipple in his mouth, and she did cry out, long and low and breathless. She moved against his thigh, wanting him to fill her *there.* Right there, where she ached. The room dissolved into a kaleidoscope of shadows and light. Before she could tell him what she needed, before she could ask him to touch her, now, she pressed upward one last time and convulsed and screamed and dissolved into the light.

The last thing she saw before giving in to the shadows was the shocked expression on Greg's taut, strained face.

WOW! HE HADN'T EXPECTED Carole's almost immediate climax. Hell, they'd just started! He'd planned to draw out the experience, building her passion, allowing her to enjoy every minute of their lovemaking.

"I'm so sorry," she whispered, burying her face in his shoulder.

"Sorry? You don't have anything to apologize for. Carole, that was fantastic. You just took me by surprise."

"You?" she laughed weakly.

He tipped her face up. "Hey, that's never happened to me before, either. I mean to anyone—"

"I think I know what you mean."

"But you know what? I don't think you're completely satisfied."

"I'm not?" She frowned as if she was testing her various body parts to get a consensus.

He cupped her breast, then skimmed his hand down her side, pulling her tight against his arousal. "I think after ten years you need more."

She smiled and turned toward him. "I think you're right."

Greg smiled in return, then lowered his head and kissed her. Slowly at first, then harder as she responded. Her enthusiasm inflamed him, making his heart beat hard and fast. His breath grew heavy against her neck, her breast, her stomach. And then he couldn't wait any longer, quickly donning a condom.

He parted her and pressed home, as slowly as possible. She was so tight and hot he had to close his eyes, lean his forehead against hers and stop moving before he lost it completely. When he had himself under control once more, he eased deeper inside. Deeper. Faster. She moved against him, clutching his back, his butt. He felt her muscles clench, vaguely heard her cry, and then joined her in the most powerful climax of his life.

THEY MUST HAVE BOTH fallen asleep, because when Carole awoke, the sun was low in the western sky. She blinked, sitting upright, wondering where she was. Why she'd taken a nap in the middle of the day. But then she remembered. She smelled the scent of freshly laundered sheets, expensive male cologne and hot, hot lovemaking.

She wouldn't be surprised to see scorch marks on the linens.

Greg stirred beside her, then opened his eyes. He didn't seem disoriented. Instead, a slow, satisfied smile spread across his face.

She yanked the sheet up to her neck, her pulse racing. Had she made a horrible mistake? What should she do now? Jump up and leave, or relax back onto the mattress? Fat chance! There was no way in the world she could relax after what she and Greg had done this afternoon.

"Hey, beautiful. Are you okay?" he asked in a sexy, husky voice.

He was the beautiful one, with his tousled dark hair, tanned, smooth skin and slightly hooded eyes. "I'm fine."

"That didn't sound very decisive."

"I don't know what to say."

He looped an arm around her neck. "I know you're not comfortable with this…situation, but it's okay. As long as you…well, as long as I didn't hurt you."

She hadn't even taken inventory of her body yet. Shifting her legs and slipping back down to the mat-

tress, she felt twinges of discomfort. Some muscles she
hadn't used in…forever. And some positions she
hadn't been in in about ten years. Maybe not then.
One thing she knew for a fact—she hadn't enjoyed
being in any position as much before.

"I'm fine." She smiled.

"You were incredible."

"Not me." He was the incredible one. "You made
me feel…wonderful. The woman you made love to
wasn't the real me. At least, that wasn't the me I've
known for twenty-eight years."

"Maybe this is the real you. Maybe you've been
waiting for the right time in your life to discover the
hidden depths of your passion."

Or maybe I've been waiting for the right man. The
thought frightened her now as much as removing her
clothes had earlier. She tried not to let her panic show
as she scooted toward the edge of the bed.

"Where are you going?"

"I…I have to go. I have chores to do." She needed
space, and time to think. She hadn't rushed into making love, but she hadn't known how she would feel,
either. And she needed to remind herself that Greg
Rafferty was not the right man for her, no matter what
her long-starved nerve endings thought.

He raised up on one elbow. "Need some help?"

"No! I mean, I just need to feed Puff," she said,
clutching the top sheet to her as she slowly pulled it
off the bed. "He'll be trying to break down the door
to the feed room. You know what they say. No rest
for the wicked," she added, attempting a little humor.
She could tell it fell flat.

"I think that's 'no rest for the weary,' and you're
running away."

"No, I told you that I have chores."

He caught her hand. "Don't, Carole. What happened here today was wonderful, not wicked. There's nothing to be ashamed of."

"I'm not ashamed. Like I said, I don't have a lot of experience with the...well, not the morning after, but close."

"Do you want more?" he asked, rubbing his thumb along the pounding pulse in her wrist.

"More?" Her heart began to race.

"More experience," he replied, his tone seductive. "Come back to bed. Then I'll help you feed that big fur ball. We can go out to dinner. I'm starving."

She was shocked that she considered his suggestion, even for an instant. "No, I can't. I really have to go." She needed to put some distance between them. A couple of miles at least. Maybe then she'd be able to think clearly. Her brain again felt like mush as he held her hands and stroked the pads of her thumbs while looking into her eyes.

"Then dinner later. After chores."

"I don't know, Greg."

"Let's go eat Mexican food. Travis and Hank told me about a place not too far from Ranger Springs, on the road to San Marcos."

"Ah, I know the place. Their food is good."

"Then let's go together. You can tell me about Jenny's camp. I'll tell you what I did in Chicago. It will be very tame, very normal."

She doubted anything about Greg could be considered "normal." He was over the top, as Cheryl would say.

He'd certainly made her go up in flames. Her face heated as she remembered how easily she'd climaxed the first time. And the second, for that matter. Despite his words of reassurance, she must have seemed very needy to him. Very unsophisticated to have been so out of control.

On the other hand, she'd already decided to have an affair with him for the duration of his visit to Ranger Springs, or until he tired of her. And in a public restaurant surely he wouldn't say anything too personal. She needed to spend more time around him so she wasn't so nervous. She couldn't have a real affair if she jumped every time he touched her.

"Okay. I'll be ready at six o'clock."

"I'll be there." He pulled her closer. "Now give me a kiss to remember you by until I see you again."

"It's only a couple of hours at the most," she said weakly, already leaning toward him.

"That's a long, long time when you're not the most patient of men."

"You're very patient," she said, surprised at the quick defense she mounted.

"No," he said with a grin, "I'm persistent. Wait until later and I'll show you."

Chapter Eleven

They ate nachos and fajitas, drank margaritas and talked until the sun set. By the time they walked hand in hand to her truck, Carole felt much more relaxed about the affair. She'd survived her decision to begin a sexual relationship, gotten naked in front of a man and responded passionately to everything they'd done.

She, single mom, dutiful daughter and respected member of the community, was involved in a hot and heavy affair with a Chicago C.E.O. Who would have imagined such a thing?

No one, she sincerely hoped. She was betting her reputation that her family, friends and neighbors didn't have a clue what she and Greg did when they were alone together.

She drove back to Ranger Springs while he told her stories about his brother and sister. Brad, it seemed, had joined the family business because it was expected and because he didn't have any other great calling. At least, none he'd shared with Greg. Stephanie loved the business almost as much as Greg, but she didn't like the operations aspect. She liked to crunch numbers and talk to bankers. Greg swore she was some kind of math whiz.

Carole couldn't identify with either of his siblings. She struggled to balance her checkbook, but did it promptly each month. She also couldn't imagine not having direction in life. A fast-growing child gave her life plenty of purpose and an equal amount of joy.

"I miss my baby," Carole said wistfully as they turned onto the rural road that led past the downtown area, out toward their respective houses.

"You mean the almost-young lady who left for camp this morning, or the baby she once was?"

Carole smiled, but she wasn't sure if Greg could see her in the dim lights of the dashboard. "Actually, I miss both of them. But I was talking about Jenny as she is now. No matter how old she is, she's still my baby."

"But you have to admit that I managed to keep your mind off her most of the day."

Carole laughed. "Yes, you did. And I suppose all your hard work was strictly for that reason."

"Well…maybe not strictly."

She heard the humor in his voice, but also the warmth. Sparing a glance at the stop sign, Carole immediately noticed that he looked darned sexy. His hair was finger combed, his shirt adorably wrinkled. The image of him lying in the rumbled bed, naked and sated, popped into her head.

"Carole?"

"Hmm?"

"Why don't you invite me home with you."

"You mean to spend the night?"

"I'd like that very much. How do you feel about sleeping together?"

"Technically, we already slept together."

"Yes, we did. I'm talking about making love, sleeping all night in the same bed and waking up together."

She took a deep breath and continued on down the road. Toward her house. Since Greg's car was at his house, no one would know that they'd driven home together. That he'd become her lover. She didn't like the idea of sneaking around but didn't have a choice. Her mother, sisters and friends might not like the idea of her sleeping with someone she'd known only a week.

However, she liked the idea a lot. Perhaps the wild teenager still lurked inside, ready for an excuse to run free. "I think I can handle that."

"If you can't, let me know. I want you to know, though, that I'd like very much to hold you tonight."

She nodded, not sure if he could see the gesture in the darkness. "You're not just saying that so I won't be alone, are you?"

"Did I seem like I was being charitable this afternoon? I don't think so. I want you. You want me. And yes, I don't want you to be all by yourself if you're going to think about how lonely you feel. I want to fill that void."

"For now. While Jenny is gone."

He let out a sigh. "Let's take this one day at a time."

"Of course. I knew that, and I didn't mean to imply anything else. I'm just…well, like I said before, I'm kind of new at this 'affair' thing."

"I know. I understand. But I want to make every minute count. And I want to wake up with you in the morning."

She remembered how safe and desired she'd felt, held tightly in his arms. Even without the great sex, the feeling was wonderful. Greg had understood her better than she'd understood herself as he'd eased her into making love. How many other men would have taken the time to talk to her, sense her hesitation and work with her fears? Not many, she'd bet. Greg was special in more ways than one.

"I want that, too," she finally said.

She seemed to feel his smile of satisfaction as the truck's headlights cut through the darkness. With luck, they'd make it back to her house without encountering any friends or neighbors who would discover what the formerly celibate mom was doing with the Yankee businessman.

GREG AWOKE SLOWLY to the bright light of morning and the feel of Carole's naked back and bottom nestled against his side. He smiled to himself, remembering how she'd led him to her bedroom. They'd undressed each other this time, taking time for hot kisses and even hotter explorations as each inch of skin was uncovered.

Carole might be a novice in the bedroom, but she was a fast learner. That must be why he felt this tenderness toward her. He'd been her first lover in ten years. She'd been as nervous as a virgin yesterday afternoon and he'd felt a responsibility to initiate her slowly and carefully.

Last night she'd taken his breath away with her exploration of his body. Especially certain parts of his body, he thought with a grin.

She stirred in her sleep, pulling the pillow down to wrap her arms around it. He eased up on one elbow and watched her settle back into sleep. Her dark brown lashes rested just above her pink flushed cheeks, lightly freckled by the Texas sun. Her lips appeared slightly swollen from his kisses, but he didn't feel any guilt. She'd enjoyed everything they'd done.

His smile faded as he realized how innocent and young Carole appeared as she lay in her queen-size bed on her pastel yellow sheets. She wasn't a sophisticated or demanding lover—the type he normally encountered. She'd approached passion with guarded enthusiasm. He could tell, without her voicing a word, that she would have liked to try even more variations on their lovemaking. She would like to be more bold. That she was unsure of her skill or his reaction made him feel even more tenderness.

But he didn't want to feel such delicate emotions. He wanted to enjoy her, make sure she enjoyed him, and move on when their time ran out. Which would be soon. He still had hopes of making her see how perfect she'd be for Huntington Foods.

Just as perfect as she'd been last night.

He eased back onto the bed, frowning at the ceiling. She wasn't perfect for him. They lived in two different worlds, had vastly different goals and different personalities. Carole was cautious, upfront and nurturing. He believed in charging ahead, carrying his cards close to his vest and doing what was best for both him and his company. She had a ten-year-old child; he'd never even thought about having children. She was from a small, close-knit town, while he'd grown up in one of the largest cities in the country where a person could walk around all day and never see anyone they knew.

No, he and Carole weren't alike. They weren't a volatile mixture like some couples he knew, but they weren't the completely compatible ideal that he'd sometimes seen. She was smart to realize all they could have together was an affair; for that, Greg was grateful. He just wished he could stay equally focused on his goals and his need to get back to Chicago as soon as possible to finalize the new ad campaign.

If he could convince Carole to be a part of Huntington's new image, so much the better. If not, he would remember her fondly.

He scooted away from her warmth and sat on the side of the bed for a few moments getting his bearings. Outside, he heard the faint but unmistakable sound of an unhappy steer. The thought of that big furry baby wanting his breakfast made Greg smile. He would feed Puff, allowing Carole more sleep, then come back in and make coffee.

After breakfast he had to get back to his real life, since the weekend, if not his working vacation, was over. He needed to call Stewart Allen, who might have news from the investigation into Carole's personal life. While looking into her background made him feel underhanded and invasive, he had to do it for the sake of his company.

If Carole was hiding a dark secret, something more than an "unfortunate incident," he needed to know before he asked her once more to become Huntington's spokesperson. If she wasn't, then no harm done. At least, as long as she didn't find out. He didn't want her to think of him as the kind of man who would both seduce her and investigate her.

He hadn't seduced her, he told himself. The sex had been mutual and the background check was just standard business procedure. He'd do the same for any potential employee who would represent Huntington Foods.

Pushing aside thoughts of his confusing personal relationship with Carole, he made himself focus once more on business. The advertising department might have some mock-ups on the ad campaign they'd discussed last week—the one that wouldn't yet feature a new spokesperson. And he needed to get current numbers on sales to see how much revenue Brad's impulsive behavior had cost the company this month.

Slipping out of bed, Greg padded softly toward the bathroom. With one last look at Carole, sound asleep in her bed, he grabbed his discarded clothes. He had chores to do and a company to run—not necessarily in that order.

WHEN CAROLE WALKED barefoot into the kitchen, Greg was sipping a cup of coffee while talking on his cell phone. He didn't notice her at first, concentrating on listening to whoever was on the line while staring out the back window. She paused in the doorway and watched him for a moment, memorizing his profile in the midmorning sunlight, noticing the golden highlights in his hair

Her attention drawn to his hand, she remembered how he'd stroked and molded and inflamed her body last night. She became a different woman when they were together, alone. For years she'd tempered her reactions, controlled her emotions and done her best to set a good example. With a stroke of his hand or a kiss from his lips, Greg changed her into someone else. Someone she didn't know. Someone who scared her senseless.

He'll be gone soon, she told herself again and again. *He's not a forever kind of guy, and besides, you wouldn't want him to be. You have a life. You have a*

daughter. You can't continue the affair, no matter how much you want him.

"That's all you could discover?" He frowned as he moved the cell phone from his right to his left ear. "Okay. Get back to me if you find out anything else."

His voice jolted her out of her daze and propelled her forward. "Good morning," she said cheerfully as she headed for the coffee.

He seemed distracted for a moment as he flipped his cell phone closed, then smiled. "Good morning. I fed Puff and made coffee." On the surface he seemed fine, but she detected some tension in his smile and posture. Business problems, no doubt.

"Thanks. I didn't mean to oversleep."

"I take full credit for exhausting you last night." He rose from the chair and walked toward her just as she reached for a mug. Her heart raced and she hoped her hands weren't trembling so much she couldn't pour a jolt of caffeine.

"In that case, you should be even more exhausted," she said with as much flippancy as possible, given the unique situation of finding a sexy man in her kitchen after a night of incredible sex. "I remember you participating, don't I?"

He settled behind her, one arm around her waist, and kissed her neck. "If you don't, I wasn't doing a good job."

"For what it's worth, I think you did a really good job." As a matter of fact, if she were paying for sex, she'd give him a big raise.

"You know what they say," he said, nuzzling aside her hair so he could nip just at the point where her neck joined her shoulder. "Nice work if you can get it."

The sensation was heavenly, awakening parts of her body the caffeine had yet to reach. Parts of her body that didn't need to be awake right now, when they both had other things to do. Besides, she didn't want to get accustomed to his touch, his kisses, when they had only days together.

"Thank you very much," she said with forced cheerfulness. "Just remember I'm a temporary employer."

His lips stopped caressing her neck; his body moved ever so slightly away. She thought she felt him stiffen, but she wasn't sure. And she wasn't going to ask. She had to keep this light. Otherwise, she'd lose it right here in her kitchen.

"Speaking of jobs, I have to go back to the house and get some work done. I have some reports being faxed to me this morning."

Carole turned around and forced a smile. "I understand. I have a few things to do as well."

He appeared more serious than before. A little more intense. "Will I see you later?"

She took a sip of coffee, almost burning her tongue. "Do you want to?"

"Absolutely."

"Why don't you come over for dinner later? Around six o'clock."

"Are you sure? We could go out."

"Not without eating fast food or pizza in town, where we'll be set upon by everyone I know, or driving to Wimberley or San Marcus. Bretford House is closed on Mondays."

"Then dinner here sounds great. Can I bring anything?"

More condoms, Carole felt like adding. "No. If I

need anything, I'll go by the grocery. I have to go to town later today." She was way behind on her baking. Customers at the café wouldn't have any coffee cake tomorrow morning or dessert after lunch today if she didn't get busy.

Greg leaned forward and brushed his lips across hers. "Later, then."

She smiled and nodded. "Thanks again for taking care of Puff."

"No problem. I'll see you at six."

GREG SETTLED back in the chair in his makeshift office and reread the report faxed by Stewart Allen. Vital statistics on Carole Lynn Jacks. Born February 3 in the Hays County Regional Hospital to parents living in Ranger Springs, Texas. Married Johnny Ray French in Arkadelphia, Arkansas and gave birth to Jennifer Lynn Jacks—not French—nine months later.

Jennifer would be eleven next month. Greg started to think about what he could get her for her birthday, but then forced his attention back to the report. He might not have a relationship with Carole or Jennifer next month.

The marriage had been annulled not even two months after she'd married the guy. Carole had been seventeen, Johnny Ray French, nineteen.

Geez, they were just kids. He counted on his fingers from the date of the wedding to the date of Jennifer's birth. Almost nine months exactly. It appeared she'd fallen for the guy, run off to Arkansas to get married, immediately got pregnant, then returned home to Ranger Springs. To her family. To have her baby.

This Johnny Ray French must be a first-class bastard, Greg thought, his hands tightening on the report.

First he takes a minor across state lines, marries her so she'll have sex with him, then leaves her when she gets pregnant because he didn't protect her. What a jerk. Carole was better off without him. No question. Jennifer, too. She didn't need a father like that. She needed...

Well, she didn't appear to need anyone. She was bright and well adjusted, polite and clever in all the ways a child should be. She didn't seem to be suffering from not having a father in her life.

Not that he was an expert on children...

Carole was younger than he and already had a ten-year old. How had she managed so well? Did she even get to finish high school? There was nothing in the report about education, so he suspected she hadn't gone to college. How could she have, raising a child with the help of her family? Her mother certainly wasn't wealthy if she still worked as a waitress at the Four Square Café. And Carole's older sister, while recently married to a prince, had gone to college part-time while working to help support the family, according to the folks he'd talked to in Ranger Springs.

He tried to keep his emotions out of this evaluation of facts, but couldn't ignore both the sympathy and admiration for Carole. She'd overcome tremendous odds and succeeded despite making a poor choice to marry at age seventeen. Or maybe it wasn't her choice. Maybe this Johnny Ray Jerk had forced himself on her and she'd insisted they marry.

Greg's tightly fisted hand crumpled the paper as he imagined Carole, alone and afraid as a teenager, either in love with or forced into intimacy by a slightly older boy. Miles away from the family and community she was so close to.

He tried to shake off the image by remembering what she'd told him. Some kind of documentary she'd been in. He'd get Stewart's investigator on that right away. He wanted to know what had been filmed or said about her. And while the P.I. was looking more closely into the past, perhaps he could find out where Carole's ex-husband lived now. Was he still a struggling musician?

If he could figure out why she was so publicity shy, maybe he could still convince her to work for Huntington. She had so much potential that was wasted in this small town.

And he had only six more days. The board of directors had called a meeting for Monday at one o'clock in the afternoon at Huntington headquarters in Chicago to discuss only one issue: the corporate image problem.

It was time to put up or shut up, as his grandfather used to say. Greg sincerely hoped he'd be able to introduce Carole Lynn Jacks, aka Ms. Carole, single mother and cookie queen extraordinaire, as their new spokesperson.

AFTER A DINNER of pork chops, mashed potatoes and green beans, Greg declined chocolate cake and, over her protests, carried her into the bedroom for what he called his own personal dessert.

Carole had anticipated the moment when they'd be together with such sharp longing that from time to time during the day, she'd stopped and closed her eyes. Greg's face, intense with passion as he moved inside her, made her stomach clench and her breasts tighten. She'd thought the days of foolish wishes and uncontrollable lust were behind her, but apparently not. Not since she'd known Greg.

Their lovemaking was slow and deliberate. She no longer needed reassurance that she was desirable or capable in the bedroom. He told her those things, and more, with each caress, each whispered encouragement and sensual groan.

As he molded her body to his, donned protection and eased inside, a verse she'd heard several years ago at a wedding sang throughout her head. *With my body, I worship thee.* Tears of joy, touched with bittersweet longing, came to her eyes as she moved with Greg, reaching for that instant when they would truly be one, if only for a moment.

She held him tightly after they could again breathe, after her brain started working.

"I'm too heavy for you."

"I love the way you feel."

"I...you feel good, too."

She rubbed her damp cheek against his shoulder. He didn't want to use the word *love*, she understood, even when talking about a physical sensation. She didn't blame him. She imagined that several women— she didn't want to think there could have been "many"—might have thought they were in love with Greg Rafferty in such a moment. She wasn't going to be jealous; they didn't have time for such negative emotions. She wanted to savor each minute together, because she would never be able to enjoy this type of relationship with him when Jenny was home.

Not that Greg was going to be around forever, she reminded herself.

"If we stay here much longer, I'm going to get you all hot and sweaty again."

"Again? So soon? Did I accidentally put an aph-rodisiac in the pork chops?"

"I think *you* are the stimulant. I can't get enough."

"Don't get addicted," she whispered against his solid shoulder.

He raised slightly, framing her face between his hands, looking down at her with tenderness. "I just might."

Oh, no. Don't start this. These feelings weren't part of the deal.

She was saved from making a comment when the phone on the nightstand rang, shattering the moment. Greg gave her one last look, then pulled away, leaving her empty and chilled in the air-conditioned room.

Carole glanced at the bedside clock—the time was nearly ten o'clock—and answered on the third ring. "Hello?" She forced her voice to sound casual, not breathless and emotionally charged.

"Carole, I was wondering if you're okay."

"Okay?" Maybe her heart was getting a little banged around on this relationship roller coaster, but she'd survive. "Sure, Mom."

"Well, I heard from Hank that the fire was getting close to his property line, and since you're so close to his ranch, I got worried about you, all alone at your place."

Chapter Twelve

"Fire?"

"The grass fire. Surely you've noticed."

"I've been inside the house." *Busy with a fire of another sort.* "What's going on? How did it start?"

"The volunteer fire department had to call other units for help to contain a grass fire that probably got started when someone tossed a cigarette out the window where the state highway turns around to the north."

"That's several miles from here."

"It's been burning for a couple of hours. Haven't you heard the fire trucks or the helicopter? One of the news stations from Austin sent their traffic copter for the ten o'clock news."

"No, I didn't hear anything." *Except the blood roaring in my ears, my heart pounding and Greg encouraging me to let everything go.* "I'm going to look outside. I'll call you back."

"Don't bother. I'm coming over, sweetie. You might need some help hosing down the barn and the roof since you're there all by yourself. See you in a few minutes."

Her mother hung up before Carole could tell her not to come. That there was already somebody here.

"What's wrong?" he asked from beside the bed. He'd apparently already made a quick trip to the bathroom and was now reaching for his clothes.

"A brush fire is moving in this direction. It's threatening Hank's property, which is next to mine."

"Is it serious?"

Carole swung her legs out of bed, her heart pounding from the adrenaline rush. "Could be, if the wind kicks up. I didn't pay any attention earlier." She'd been thinking of Greg, only Greg, as she'd fixed dinner, bathed and turned down the bed. "My mother is on her way over."

"Damn," he muttered. He looked up. "I don't want to leave you alone, but what if she sees my car?"

His rental was parked around back, near the barn, where it wouldn't be noticed by anyone from the road but would be unmistakable to anyone hosing down the wooden structure.

He pulled aside the curtain at the window and peered into the darkness. A faint red tinged the horizon. "You might need more help than your mother can provide."

"I don't—"

Before she could tell him that she and her mother could handle the potential problem, someone pulled into her driveway. A red flashing light, making a strobe effect on her drawn curtains, told her this visitor wasn't her mother.

"Damn," she muttered, reaching for her panties. She wasn't dressed. She needed to be dressed and outside *now,* before a fire official or neighbor assumed she wasn't home and tried to move Puff out of the barn.

"Carole!" a man's voice called out.

"Oh, no."

"Who is that?" Greg asked.

"Pastor Carl Schleipinger. He's apparently making the rounds for the volunteer fire department, alerting the homes that might be threatened. I need to get dressed!"

"I'll get the door."

"No!"

"You want to ignore him?"

She wanted to shout "yes" as she struggled to locate her shorts and T-shirt. Where had she thrown them earlier?

Pastor Carl pounded on her door. "Carole, are you home?"

She groaned as she looked up at Greg, already dressed. "Okay, answer the door. We'll deal with explanations later."

He didn't say another word, just turned and walked out of the bedroom. She didn't dare turn on a light because that would tell Pastor Carl where she was. What she and Greg had been doing. Why the lights were out.

Groaning, she grabbed her clothes and hurried into the bathroom to dress. When she emerged a couple of minutes later, she heard her mother's concerned voice drifting down the hallway.

Great. Carole couldn't imagine a worse scenario than her mother and her pastor talking to her lover in her darkened living room at ten o'clock at night.

She took a deep breath, clutched the stack of towels to her chest and hurried toward the voices.

"Mom, Pastor Carl. What's going on with the fire?"

"It's not moving very fast, but we decided to alert everyone in the area so you could take precautions," Pastor Carl replied. "Move any firewood or brush away from your house or barn, wet down the roof and get any animals ready to evacuate if it gets worse."

"I didn't know you had company," her mother said.

"You didn't give me time to tell you that Greg had come by for supper so we could talk about his company."

Her mother glanced at the wall clock. It was after ten o'clock. She raised an eyebrow.

Carole decided to ignore her. "Thank you so much, Pastor Carl. How many more houses are you visiting?"

"There's just about four more on the road. We don't think the fire will get this far, but better be careful."

"Right. I was just going to wet down these towels in case we need them. I wasn't sure how smoky the air might get."

"I'll be going," Pastor Carl said. "Y'all be safe tonight."

"Oh, we will be," Greg replied. *He was probably thinking of safe sex,* Carole thought.

"Maybe we'll see you at services on Sunday," the pastor said, opening the front door. He didn't know that Greg would be gone soon. But she didn't have time to think about that now.

Carole attempted a smile. "Good night, Pastor Carl."

"If you'll show me what to do, I'll get started hosing down the roof. Or whatever else you need,'' Greg offered as soon as the door closed.

''Mom, can you turn on the outside lights? Greg can make sure everything is moved away from the house while you and I start on the barn. I'll get Puff's halter and lead rope on him just in case we have to move him out. I'll also hook up the trailer and pull it into the driveway.''

''Okay. Oh, and sweetie, you might want to gather your photos and important papers,'' her mother said, shrugging. ''Just in case.''

Carole nodded, dropping her stack of towels on the kitchen table and hurrying into the family room. While she placed photo albums and scrapbooks into a tote bag, she noticed the lights coming on outside. Through the windows she heard her mother and Greg talking. *Please, Lord, don't let her quiz him about me. I want to keep this simple.*

She knew she wasn't good at having an affair. But she didn't have time to think about that now. Grass and brush fires in the summer were a fact of life. Some were caused by lightning, but most were caused by careless people. Smokers, outdoor cooks, campers. Arsonists.

She didn't have time to think about that, either. She went to the file cabinet and placed her important papers in the tote. Her property deed, investment accounts and one very important paper dissolving her brief marriage.

She paused for a moment, remembering how she'd paid little attention to the details at the time her mother had petitioned the court on her behalf. She'd been too involved in her own angst, worrying about what everyone thought of her, how she looked and how she was going to care for a baby. She'd been so young, so stupid. Those days seemed like a lifetime ago.

She'd considered putting the baby up for adoption, but her family had appeared appalled by the idea. Kerry had sworn they'd get through it together, that they were family and would all pitch in. The baby was family, too, her sisters reminded her, and deserved to be raised right here.

Carole was so glad she'd listened to her heart. Jenny had made the family stronger. She'd made Carole stronger, too, by forcing her to grow up.

Just like Greg had made her stronger by making her face her fear of intimacy. Sexual intimacy. He'd blown away the last vestige of that shallow, superficial girl who'd taken far too much pride in how she filled out her Wranglers.

Shaking away thoughts of Greg, she focused once more on the crisis at hand. She wasn't about to let Jenny's home burn, she thought, pushing to her feet. She had a truck to move, a trailer to hitch and a mother's questions to avoid.

GREG STRETCHED the kinks from his back as he settled into the kitchen chair. At the counter Carole and her mother, Charlene, were fixing coffee. Dawn had just broken. The fire was contained, straying only slightly onto Carole's property after the volunteer fire department used water from her stock tank—which was really a man-made pond—to put it out. Only three fence posts had been charred by the flames.

Of course, they all bore remnants of the night. Their clothes smelled of smoke, they were sweaty, tired and hungry. He needed coffee, food and a shower—preferably with Carole after her mother went home.

"Are you sure I can't go get breakfast? The fast-food place has a drive-through, don't they?"

"Yes, but that's not necessary," Charlene answered. "We can fix something here in a jiffy."

"Mama, don't you have to get to work?" Carole asked as she removed mugs from the cabinet.

"Yes, but I wanted to make sure everything was fine at your place. I couldn't go off to the café not knowing what was happening."

Greg sincerely hoped Charlene meant about the fire, not about him.

"As you can see, we're fine."

"Yes, but—"

"And Greg is here in case any embers pop up or there's another problem."

Charlene poured coffee, ignoring her daughter's question. "Cream or sugar?" she asked, turning toward Greg.

"No, thanks. Black is fine."

She placed the mug on the table in front of him with a strained smile. "Greg, how long are you going to be in town?"

"I have to be back in Chicago for a Monday-afternoon board meeting."

"I see." She turned to Carole. "That's not very long."

"No, but I can always come back," he added.

"And I'm sure you'd be welcome. But really, your life is in Chicago, right?"

Carole spun around. "Mama, that's not even the least bit subtle. I know Greg's life is in Chicago, but he's here now. Let's just leave it at that."

Charlene sighed. "I will if you can."

Greg watched Carole's face, noticing a flash of pain

in her tense features and blue-gray eyes. "Of course. Greg and I have a professional relationship. I'm still Ms. Carole, after all," she said with a forced laugh.

The coffee settled in his stomach like acid as he listened to her false bravado. He couldn't be a by-stander to any more subtle confrontation between mother and daughter. He jumped from his chair and walked toward Carole.

"We have more than a professional relationship, Mrs. Jacks. I care about your daughter, but you're right—my job and my life are in Chicago. She knows that. We've been honest with each other." He placed his arm around Carole's shoulders and pulled her close. "I'm only here temporarily, but that doesn't mean we can't have an adult relationship."

Charlene took a deep breath. "I know. You're right. I'm just meddling," she said, sweeping her arm in a dismissive gesture. "I don't have a lot of experience as a meddling mother."

Carole eased away and put her arms around her mother. "It's okay, Mama. I'm not seventeen any-more. I know what I'm doing."

"I know you do. But when I came here tonight, thinking you were all alone, and Greg was here with you and I'd obviously interrupted something—"

"Actually, Pastor Carl almost interrupted some-thing," Carole corrected.

"That's even worse."

"It's not better or worse," Greg pointed out. "That's just what happened. Carole and I were having a wonderful evening and then there was a fire. That's all anyone needs to know."

"I'm not worried about anyone else!" Charlene ex-claimed. "I'm just thinking of Carole."

"I'm fine, Mama. Don't worry about me. I'm a big girl now."

He supposed this was the part of an awkward conversation where, if there was a father involved, he asked the "young man" about his intentions toward his daughter. But there wasn't a father because he'd split years ago, leaving Charlene and the three girls alone. Greg could understand why they'd all have an issue with men who were here today, gone tomorrow.

"Whatever our personal or professional relationship, I hope to see Carole in the future. I would never do anything to hurt her or Jennifer. I care about them both."

"Then that's fine with me. Carole is right. You two are both adults. Jenny is away at camp, and what you do when you're alone isn't anyone else's business. I don't know what got into me."

"You're just tired, Mama. You've been up all night."

"We're all tired," Greg said. And he still wanted something to eat, a shower and Carole beside him while he slept.

"I'm going to take my coffee 'to go,' grab a shower and call the café. Maybe I do need to take the day off."

"That's an excellent idea."

"Why don't we all go out to dinner tonight?" Greg suggested. "You and Cheryl could join us at Bretford House."

"That's a nice idea. I'll ask her. I don't think she has any appointments for her petting zoo on a weeknight." She gathered up her purse and car keys. "I'll talk to you later, sweetie."

"Later, Mama," Carole said, giving her mother another hug.

The kitchen door whooshed shut, filling the house with blessed silence. Suddenly awkward silence.

Carole turned to look at him, her expression unreadable. "So, you're leaving on Sunday."

SHE KNEW he was leaving soon, just not when. As long as she didn't know the exact day, she could ignore the warning bells in her head that rang out "watch your heart" over and over again.

"I have to go back to Chicago. The board has called a meeting to discuss what we're doing about the crisis."

"You mean about the mess Brad caused."

"A mess, yes, but one we must clean up soon. I've taken some interim steps with a revised ad campaign, but we still need a spokesperson."

She felt her heart pound in her chest. Her blood pressure must be through the roof. First the fire, then their "discovery," and now this revelation.

"I told you I wouldn't do it."

"Have I asked you lately?" he said, clearly irritated. His hands were on his hips and his expression was one she hadn't seen in a while. Acute frustration tinged with a bit of a challenge.

"No, but I... Oh, I don't know what I meant."

"I think you've said 'no' so much that it's a programmed response."

"That's not true!"

"Really?"

"No! I just don't like to be pushed into a corner. I also don't like to be talked about. And I'm still tense about people showing up when you were here, with the lights out, around bedtime.''

"You think your pastor or your mother are going to run back to Ranger Springs with tales of you doing the wild thing with a Chicago businessman who's just in town for a few days?''

"No, of course not.''

"Then what's the problem?''

She wanted to scream. Instead, she ran her hands through her messy hair and pressed her thumbs against her throbbing temples. "I don't know. I'm too tired to think.''

With her eyes closed and her head pulsing, she didn't hear Greg walk up. But suddenly he was there, wrapping his strong arms around her, pulling her against his chest.

"I'm not trying to corner you into doing anything, Carole. I'm also not trying to flaunt our relationship. It's no one's business but our own.'' His hands lifted hers away from her head and placed them around his neck. Then he massaged her tense shoulders and neck until she was practically purring like her mama's cat.

"We've had a long, long night. Let's take a shower and get some sleep. Things will look better in the morning. Or, in this case, the afternoon.''

"You're probably right,'' she said, her voice muffled against his smoke-scented chest. "I'm so tired I don't know if I can stand upright in the shower.''

"Then let me help.''

Before she could think about what he meant, he swung her into his arms and strode down the hall toward the master bath. She briefly thought about protesting, but couldn't gather the energy. Besides, being held in his arms, having him take over the decision making for a while, felt heavenly.

When he put her down, she leaned against the cool tile wall and started to undress. He turned on the water, then quickly stripped, which she watched from the corner of her eye. He looked so darn good, all firm golden skin and subtle sculpted muscles. Long, swimmer muscles, not the weight-lifter kind. She sighed in appreciation.

"What?" he asked, turning toward her as he stripped away his jeans.

"I really enjoy looking at you," she said with another sigh. She probably shouldn't have admitted something like that—sophisticated women no doubt would have kept their mouths shut—but she didn't have the strength to guard her feelings right now.

Greg grinned. "The feeling is mutual. I really like looking at you." He eyed her half-unbuttoned shirt and unsnapped jeans. "Speaking of which, I'm way ahead of you again. Time to catch up."

She smiled as she finished undressing. The light of the frosted-glass window admitted early-morning sunlight, making her hope he got in the shower quickly. She still felt uncomfortable being naked around him in the light. However, she should have known Greg wouldn't do as she wished.

"Come here," he said softly, standing by the tub, the shower curtain pulled back to reveal wisps of steam from the gentle setting of her showerhead.

She stepped into his arms, then looked into his eyes. He might be a temporary lover, but she would remember the caring look in his eyes forever. "A few days ago I didn't want to take my clothes off in front of you. I was too worried about how I looked."

"I know, but I still don't understand. You have a great body."

"I have the body of an almost-thirty-year-old woman. I was still trying to live up to the ideal of a teenager."

"Teenagers are highly overrated, especially by themselves."

"Oh, come on. Tell me you've never ogled those perky, nubile singers in low hip-huggers and minuscule halter tops."

Greg shook his head. "Never. Not ogling, anyway. More in wonder. Like I wonder how much is real and how much was surgically enhanced."

"I know, but I'd love to have my pre-stretch-mark figure."

"You can barely tell you've ever been pregnant," he said, sweeping his hands down her hips, his thumbs coming to rest on her hipbones. "And besides, I love knowing you carried Jennifer inside you. It's so... miraculous."

"Oh, Greg." She leaned toward him, kissing him with all the emotion she felt. Perhaps she wasn't thinking clearly at the moment, but she imagined she saw love in his eyes. She imagined that she felt the same in her heart.

He broke away first, his desire evident despite swearing he was exhausted. He didn't feel as if he'd been up all night, soaking her barn and roof, moving her stack of firewood to a safe location. He felt... wonderful.

"Let's get in before the water turns cold," she suggested.

"Good idea. Besides, if we wait much longer, no

telling who might come to the door. This way, we can at least honestly say that you were in the shower.''

She laughed until he pressed her against the wet tiles, kissed her senseless and found new uses for the bath puff and scented soap Cheryl had given her for Christmas.

Chapter Thirteen

After they had made love and slept until a little after noon, Greg had gone back to his house. Carole felt filled with restless energy after waking, both from the erratic schedule and the thoughts of Greg that kept spinning inside her head like a dog chasing its own tail.

She loved being with him when they were together, alone, but when she thought about her family and friends speculating on the relationship, she panicked. She didn't want people saying that she was repeating a past mistake, falling for the wrong man. A man who wouldn't be around in both good times and bad. A man who had a life that didn't include a small-town woman with only a high school education, a ten-year-old daughter and a career baking cookies.

She'd been wrong to throw his quest for a spokesperson in his face. He wasn't badgering her to agree any longer. They were just having a brief affair, and then he would leave. Perhaps they would see each other again, but she doubted the relationship would be the same. How could it, when the intensity grew the longer they were around each other? Absence didn't make the heart grow fonder, from her experience. Absence made the heart grow cold.

She used her nervous energy to bake coffee cakes and cookies for the Four Square Café, plus made some extra dough to freeze for when Jenny came home from camp. She'd take the baked goods to town later, perhaps when they went to dinner.

Did Greg really like the people in Ranger Springs, or was he just tolerating them for her sake? She wished she knew more about men. Maybe about the way an adult "dating" relationship worked. Her lack of experience was showing in more than the bedroom. She wondered if Greg minded that she was ignorant of many of the skills other women possessed.

There were so many ways they were different, but she wanted him to be satisfied. To be happy. And although she seemed to please him when they were alone, he had to be accustomed to more of everything. More restaurants. Nightclubs. Health clubs. Whatever a big city offered, Ranger Springs lacked. Not that he was going to spend a lot of time here.

She sighed, taking the last batch of cookies from the oven. She had to stop worrying about Greg. About them. He was going back to Chicago this coming weekend. They had a few days left. Tonight they'd have dinner, then come home to the empty house. She wanted them to enjoy these stolen moments together, to make the memories last, because she had a sinking feeling in her stomach that even if she waited another ten years for a man, she wouldn't find one as handsome, kind, intelligent and interesting as Greg Rafferty.

DINNER STARTED OUT WELL, but then several people came by the table to ask about the fire. How much of her land had damage? Was her fence down? Did flames get close to the house? Greg sat through each question, keeping his silence because he didn't want to reveal that he was at Carole's house through the night. He knew she'd be mortified if she thought people were whispering behind her back.

Even now, several friends and neighbors were glancing at the table. He recognized the Branson man from the hardware store at one table, the banker and his wife at another. They nodded, smiled slightly and went back to their food when they noticed him watching them. Friendly, not condemning, as Carole would assume.

If only she didn't have this fear of public attention. She'd be the perfect woman…for Huntington, of course. She could gain confidence by having professionals style her, and when she saw herself on tape, she'd know how perfect she was to extol the virtues of Ms. Carole's cookies. How qualified she was to tell the public that Huntington produced a good, healthy product meant to be consumed in moderation as part of the American diet.

He had to talk to her again, despite his personal vow to enjoy the time they had together fully. Carole deserved one more chance to change her mind, to make a difference in her life and Jennifer's future. With the money she'd earn as spokesperson, there would be no more need to show cattle at the 4-H events to earn enough for college. Carole could buy a bigger house, or remodel her kitchen or give her mother enough so she'd never have to work again. She could travel more, perhaps visit her sister in Europe or go to places she'd never seen. The world would open up if only she'd agree to his plan.

Hell, he wasn't asking her to lie. Just talk about her recipes and the quality cookies Huntington Foods produced.

"Greg, would you like dessert?"

Charlene Jacks's question startled him out of his thoughts of Carole and what might be. Or what might never be.

"I'm pretty full."

"You didn't eat much," Carole commented.

He'd barely tasted the pot roast and potatoes he'd eaten automatically. "I'm fine. Go ahead and order dessert if you'd like."

The ladies declined, so he gestured for the check. Within minutes they were making their way through the tables, saying hello to other folks and exclaiming that yes, the fire was sure exciting. And with every step, he felt more and more determined to talk to Carole again. Perhaps this time she'd listen to reason.

"WOULD YOU LIKE some dessert now? Maybe some coffee?" Carole asked as she placed her purse and keys on the kitchen table.

"No, thanks. I'm not hungry."

He shut and locked the door, then walked to where she stood, his expression unreadable. Throughout dinner she'd felt he had something on his mind. He'd been unusually quiet during their drive home, too. And the Greg she knew would have made some sexual innuendo about "dessert" and "hungry," but he'd passed up the opportunity.

"What's wrong, Greg?"

"I want to talk to you. Can we sit down in the living room?"

"Of course." She tried not to get too nervous about his subdued tone of voice, his rather stiff body language.

She sat on the couch, clutching her hands as he paced, then settled next to her.

"I want to talk to you about Huntington, but I don't want you to get all defensive again. I really need you to keep an open mind about becoming the spokesperson."

His words rankled, immediately making her pull away.

"That's exactly what I'm talking about. I don't know how to approach this subject, Carole. Every time I mention—"

"That's because we have nothing to talk about. I don't know why you can't accept my answer, which, in case you've forgotten, is 'No.'"

"But why? You are everything the public would love. A single mother successfully raising a child. You are articulate yet soft-spoken. I'll bet my life you're extremely photogenic, from what I've seen of the pictures around the house of you and Jennifer. And you are the real thing—a person who took her skills and turned them into a multimillion dollar product line for us."

"You are forgetting the negatives. I'd be open to criticism about being a single mother, about not having a higher education, about producing the type of product that made the C.A.S.H.E.W. people attack Huntington in the first place."

"You could give us a new, healthy cookie recipe. You mentioned you might have one."

"That doesn't eliminate the other problems!"

"Those are only problems in your mind. You're playing a game of 'what if' with yourself. I've told you there are ways we could protect you from such criticism."

"You can't protect me from everything, Greg!" she nearly shouted, jumping from the couch. She walked to the stack of photo albums she'd brought in from the truck earlier. The ones she'd wanted to protect in case the fire threatened the house. She stared down at them, her arms wrapped around her middle as a physical pain clenched her in a tight fist.

"What's wrong, Carole? Please, talk to me."

She reached down, pulling out a purple album with various brightly colored stickers on the front and spine. Jennifer's early attempt at art, she remembered with bittersweet emotions. "While the cookies were baking earlier, I took a look at this album. Jenny's scrapbook. I didn't know she'd been adding to it recently. She kept that information from me, I suppose, because she thought my feelings would be hurt."

"What's in the scrapbook?"

"Photos of her father."

"I thought you didn't have a relationship with him. What's his name? Johnny Ray…something?"

She spun around, clutching the scrapbook. "How did you know that?" No one around here talked about him.

Greg shrugged. "We had to know if you were right for the position."

"So you did what? Had me investigated?"

"No more than we would have done for any other employee in a key position. Just a standard background check."

"Yes, but I'm not an employee, am I, Greg? I never wanted to be one. I was perfectly happy licensing my cookie recipes to you until you came to Texas and tried to talk me into doing things I could never do."

He jumped up from the couch. "Were you perfectly happy, Carole, or were you hiding from life? You can't be happy if you're living in fear."

"I'm not afraid! I'm careful. I have responsibilities!"

"Yes, you do, and one of those is to provide a good example to your daughter. Do you tell her she can be whatever she wants to be when she grows up?"

"Of course." She clutched the scrapbook tighter. Jenny's scrapbook. The daughter who now had secrets, too.

"And what kind of example are you showing her? That it's okay to be afraid of life? That you really can't be whatever you want to be because it's okay to be afraid?"

She trembled with rage, the album edges biting into her palms. "That's enough. I don't have to listen to you!"

"No, you don't, but I want you to listen to yourself. You're afraid, Carole, and I don't know why. I care about you. I want to know."

"You want to know?" She stalked to the couch and, using both hands, plunked the scrapbook down in front of him. "Let me show you." She flipped quickly through the first dozen pages of the book. Pages filled with photos of Jenny and her stuffed animals. Jenny and her pets. Jenny and her friends at birthday parties. Then ribbons and programs from school and 4-H, more photos, more mementos.

And then, the newest pages. Photos of a man, cut

out of a magazine. Articles about him. "This is my secret, Greg. This is why I need to be private."

"A country-western singer?"

She backed away from the coffee table, her hand covering her chin and mouth as tears stung her eyes. "Johnny Ray French. Jennifer's father."

"He's famous?"

Carole laughed, a sound almost a sob. "Yes, he is now. Ten years ago he was just a member of a band. A talented but immature boy who didn't want a wife or child. He wanted bright lights and fame, wild women and alcohol. He certainly didn't want a small-town bride who'd gotten knocked up in a cheap motel room in Arkansas because she thought she couldn't get pregnant the first time she 'did it.'"

"He was your husband," Greg said softly.

Carole shook her head. "He was the boy I married. He was never a husband. He's never been a father."

"Then what's the problem? You have each gone your own way. Jennifer is well adjusted."

"Do you think the press would let this story lie if I got in the spotlight? They'd ask him all types of intrusive questions. What was it like being married to Ms. Carole? Did she bake cookies for you back then? What type of role do you play in your daughter's life? How do you think he's going to react to being ambushed by reporters for something he'd put behind him more than ten years ago?"

"Not well, I assume."

"Darn right! He's going to be furious. If it's reported that he's never had contact with his own daughter, never paid a dime of child support, what will the public say about him? What will his record label do to him?"

"I see your point."

"Finally!" she exclaimed, throwing up her hands.

"Carole, this is the first time you've told me about your ex-husband. You refused to talk about him. That's one reason I asked someone responsible and discreet to find out as much as possible about the facts of your life."

"Oh! That is so intrusive."

"It's necessary in business."

"I'm not going to be part of your business."

"Carole, just listen to me. We can overcome this problem with your ex-husband by approaching him privately. This doesn't have to hurt you or Jennifer."

"Of course it will hurt her. Look at this scrapbook!" she said, sweeping her hand across the evidence of her daughter's secret fascination. "I didn't know she had these magazines. We don't listen to his music in this house. We don't talk about him. And now she has him in this scrapbook. How do you think she'll feel when she knows we talked to him, told him about this publicity you have planned, and he says he still wants nothing to do with his daughter?"

"We can keep Jennifer out of this."

"No we can't! Because you know what else could happen? He could decide that having no contact with his daughter would be worse than being a father. What if he decides to take a role in her life? Or maybe take her away from me?"

She leaned close, across the coffee table, close enough to see the gold flecks in his blue-green eyes. "Can you absolutely guarantee that the courts won't allow him access to Jenny? Or that she won't decide to…to go live with her father? The man she's documented in this book. The man with lots of money and fame. That's what I'm competing against, Greg, and there's no way in hell you can guarantee that Jenny will be able to live a normal life here in Ranger Springs if her father becomes part of her life.''

GREG KNEW he couldn't talk to Carole when she was so upset, but he had the strongest urge to hold her in his arms, stroke her hair and tell her everything was going to be fine. She'd rebuffed him when he'd tried. She wanted nothing to do with him after he caused her such pain. He'd brought out every secret fear, every horrible scenario that she'd probably never voiced before.

He leaned back against the couch in his rented home and hugged a pillow to his chest, wishing she were here. She shouldn't be alone tonight. But what could he do? He was the last person in the world she wanted to see after she'd revealed her secret.

Parts of the puzzle that was Carole Jacks had fallen into place, though, when he'd learned her greatest fear—losing her daughter to the ''idealized'' father in those glossy magazines. Carole had mentioned a documentary, one he imagined had something to do with Johnny Ray French—the early years. Perhaps even when Carole was still with him, before Jennifer was born. He'd asked Stewart to find more about the film, but apparently it was obscure, buried in the depths of some film vault. Probably not even indexed, or it would have been shown when French became famous.

Someone would have dragged out the dirty linen, just like disreputable journalists would like to do on Ms. Carole herself if she were to become a spokesperson.

But was there any dirty linen? He didn't think so,

although he had to admit he still wasn't thinking too straight about her. He wanted to be objective, but he kept seeing her ravaged face, the fear in her eyes. He hated that he'd caused her to imagine such terrible scenarios.

She shouldn't be alone. When Jennifer had first left for camp, Carole had said how she hated to be alone in the house. How she missed her daughter's giggles and complaints and everything that went with a ten-year-old girl.

He grabbed the pillow and threw it across the room. Dammit, he had to do *something*. Jumping to his feet, he paced to the phone. He might not be able to comfort her, but he knew someone who could.

"So Greg called Hank to get my number, and he called me to come over, sweetie. Hank said Greg was so upset."

"Sure," Carole said, hugging her mother so hard she'd probably have bruises tomorrow. "I think he finally realized I meant no. He's probably packing right now."

"I don't think so. I think he really cares."

"Then why does he keep pushing me, Mama? Why can't he leave everything alone?"

"Because he's trying to do what he thinks is right for his company, just like you're trying to do what you think is best for yourself and Jenny."

"I don't think, I *know*. How could exposing her to either a public rebuff by her father or an attempt to take her away from her family be okay?"

"You don't know that's what will happen."

"Ha!" she said, pulling away and sniffing into her damp tissue. "You don't know Johnny Ray."

"Sweetie," her mother said, taking her by the shoulders, "neither do you. At least, not the way he is now. You only knew him as a nineteen-year-old loser. He's about thirty now, a successful musician who has a pretty good reputation."

"How do you know that?"

"I read more than the royalty magazines, Carole Lynn," her mother said, giving her a parental look that used to make her cringe. It still worked. She sniffed again and twisted away to pace the room.

"Did you see this scrapbook? Jenny did this all on her own. I didn't even know!"

"She's growing up. Of course she's curious about her father."

"She should have asked me."

"Carole, once again, I have to tell you that you don't know anything about the man he is today. You only know the boy you married."

"He was a jerk."

"Yes, he was, and you were a silly teenager. But look at you now. You're responsible and successful and you're a wonderful mother."

Carole felt as though her heart was being twisted inside her chest. "I had an affair with Greg, Mama. How responsible was that?"

"Oh, Carole."

"Exactly! I was stupid again."

"That's not what I meant! I don't think making the decision to have a relationship with Greg is stupid. He isn't Johnny Ray, sweetie. And your private life is your business. You should enjoy yourself."

"How can you say that? You're my mother!"

She shrugged. "He's a very good-looking man and he obviously cares about you. You weren't hurting anyone, so it's not up to me to say you did anything wrong.''

"Pastor Carl may disagree with you."

"Well now, you'll have to take that up with him. I decided long ago that I would love you girls just as much when you became adults as I did when you were children. And believe me, an adult child can be just as difficult as a little one. Why, at one point, Kerry even accused me of wanting her to marry Alexi because he was a prince! Now, I know that's not true, and she did apologize, but she was talking out of fear, just like you."

"That's completely different. She was pregnant with his baby, and you have to admit that you always liked him."

"Yes, I did, and I love him like a son now. That's why I think you should talk to your sister about this. She, better than anyone, would have some insights into dealing with the public...and insistent men, for that matter."

Carole held her head between her hands as her whole world spun around and around, so fast and crazy that she couldn't get her bearings. She didn't want to deal with the public. She didn't want to tell her entire family about her recent mistake. "I can't believe this night. I can't believe this conversation."

Her mother pulled her down to the couch, sitting beside her and putting an arm around her shoulders. The world slowed and stopped wobbling so much. "Carole, you're an adult, but you'll always be my daughter. Someday you'll have to say those same words to Jennifer. And I know you will, because no matter what difficulties come between you, there's nothing like the love of a mother for her daughter. So

I know you're hurting by what seems like a betrayal from Jenny, but it's just her way of expressing herself. She didn't want to upset you, so she kept it a secret. Don't make too much of her actions. And don't worry about Johnny Ray. He's a small part of your past. He doesn't have to be part of your future.''

"You can't know that. Greg can't know that, although he tried to tell me the same thing earlier. I think you're both glossing over the very real possibility that Jenny's father will interfere in our lives.''

"Well, we just don't know, now, do we?''

"The only way to know for sure is to remain here in Ranger Springs, nice and quiet, just as we've been for the past ten years. If Jenny wants to find her father later, when she's older, that's her choice. But I won't expose her to hurt when I don't have to.''

Her mother sighed. "I hear what you're saying, but it all boils down to the fact that you're afraid of what *might* happen. I just hate to think of you being so scared.''

"I'm not scared all the time, Mama.'' Just when she thought about losing her daughter. Losing her well-ordered life among family and friends.

Losing her one and only lover.

"You and Greg need to talk about this when you're not so upset over Jennifer and Johnny Ray.''

Carole shook her head, the idea of talking to Greg again even more upsetting than thinking about the past. "Greg made his intentions clear in the beginning, when he wanted me to be the spokesperson for Huntington Foods. And that would have been fine, but then I went and…and I wanted him, Mama. We were so attracted to each other that I wanted to believe he was coming back to Ranger Springs just for me. Just for *me,*" she repeated, thumping her chest with her fist as she saw her life, her mistakes, so clearly.

"And then he came back and he was so nice to Jenny. She thinks he's great," Carole said, sniffing. "So I went to him and forgot all about the fact he still wanted me to be the spokesperson. He kept complimenting me on how well I handled problems, what good ideas I had and other things I realize now were all about subtle manipulation.

"It wasn't about me, the woman, Mama. It was always about his company."

"I don't believe that's true. We've all seen the way Greg looks at you. He's not *that* good an actor."

"You just don't know him well."

"Carole Lynn, neither do you."

"And now I never will!" Because she had terrible taste in men. Because men couldn't be trusted to love someone enough to be there through good times and bad. Because even the good ones, like Greg had seemed to be, were no better than her father or her former husband.

She turned to her mother, hugged her tight, and burst into a new set of tears.

Chapter Fourteen

"Did you have a good time at camp?" Carole asked as Jenny trooped to the front door on Saturday morning just before noon, dragging her duffel behind her.

"It was neat. We caught those little green snakes and put them in the boys' cabin. And we went swimming every day. Meagan got poise and ivy, and Ashley threw up after she ate too many cupcakes one night. That was yucky."

"Wow," Carole said, forcing her best cheerful voice. She knew she should tell her daughter that Meagan had "poison ivy," and terrifying boys with snakes wasn't very nice, and eating too many cupcakes could make anyone sick, but she didn't have the energy. Ever since talking to her mother, realizing what a mistake she'd made this time regarding a man, she just didn't feel up to worrying about the little things.

"You look really tired, Mom," Jenny said as Carole held the door open for her.

"Well, we had a little excitement around here the night before last."

"The fire?"

"How did you know?"

"We saw it from the road, and Ashley's mother told

us there was a grass fire at Mr. Whittaker's place and part of Uncle Hank's property.''

"That's right. And we got a little burned, but not much. Just a little grass and a couple of fence posts.''

"Is Puff okay? He didn't get scared, did he?''

"No, he's fine. Grandma came over, and so did Mr. Rafferty, so I had lots of help.''

"Oh, that's good. So, why are you so tired?''

Carole dragged Jenny's duffel into the laundry room, tempted to dump the whole thing in the washing machine. "I stayed up all night just to make sure the fire didn't get too close to the house or barn.''

"Oh." Jenny looked around the kitchen. "Do you have any cookies?''

"Yes, I do. I made your favorite.''

"Chunky chocolate chip! Yeah!''

Carole managed a weak smile as her daughter rushed into the kitchen. She focused on the dirty clothes, telling herself that things would be fine now. Jenny was home for the summer, except for short trips or sleepovers. The house wouldn't be empty anymore.

"So is Mr. Rafferty coming over today? I want to show him my friendship bracelet," Jenny said from the doorway, holding out her arm.

Carole took a deep breath. "Mr. Rafferty isn't coming over. I imagine he's already gone back to Chicago.''

"Oh," Jenny said, deflated. "I wanted to see him. When is he coming back?''

"I don't think he's coming back.''

"What?" Jenny sounded incredulous, as if she couldn't imagine life without Greg Rafferty. "Why did he go away? Where's Puff? What did he do with him?''

"He didn't do anything…yet." Except leave the big steer here for Jennifer, along with a six-month supply of grain that would barely fit in the feed room and an equal supply of hay was stored in an empty stall. Lester Boggs at the feed store said he had instructions to deliver more if needed and charge it to Greg. Of course, being Lester, he'd said it with a wink that implied the Chicago businessman had ulterior motives for being so generous.

Lester didn't have a clue. No one did. They all thought Greg was romancing her by being nice to her family and friends, buying Jenny's steer and providing feed, and spending so much time in Ranger Springs. Ha!

But she didn't want to think about Greg. She wanted to answer her daughter's question and focus on her return from camp. "Mr. Rafferty said that if we didn't want to keep Puff, he would make arrangements to put him in a petting zoo. I think he found one in Fort Worth that would take him."

"Puff doesn't want to live in Fort Worth, around a bunch of strangers."

"Sometimes we don't have a lot of choices," Carole said quietly, sorting colored clothes from whites that needed bleach. She turned her head to the wall, but she could tell Jenny was watching her.

"Mom, you look really weird. What's wrong?"

Carole sniffed. "I'm fine. I just don't want to talk about Mr. Rafferty anymore, okay?"

"Are you mad at him?"

"No, I'm not mad." She measured detergent, then closed the lid and turned on the washer. "Well, maybe a little angry."

"What did he do?"

Carole wanted to wave off her daughter's question, but knew the subject would come up again. "You know how he wanted me to work for his company? Well, when he came back, he kept bringing it up and finally we had a big fight."

"What did he want you to do?"

"Put my picture on the packages of cookies, make commercials, speak to people. That sort of thing." She shrugged. "That's just not me, Jenny. I can't do things like that."

"Why?"

"Because people who make commercials and do interviews on television and things like that are...different."

"How?"

"What is this, twenty questions? Just trust me that I couldn't do what he wanted, and he didn't understand that."

"But, Mom, you always said that a person can be whatever they want to be. I think it would be fun to be famous and be on TV. Why wouldn't you want to do that?"

"Because then people start talking about you. Maybe they don't like the way you wear your hair or the clothes you wear. Or they think you talk stupid or laugh at your accent. And then they won't buy cookies because if they don't like me, they don't like the cookies."

"I don't think there are many people like that. I think people would really like you, Mom."

"I'm not a celebrity, Jenny."

"Well, you could be, if you wanted to. I don't understand why you wouldn't want to see your picture on the cookie bags. That would be so neat to show my friends.''

Jenny didn't understand how disruptive such publicity would be. She couldn't imagine the downside of being a celebrity—if you could call someone who came up with cookie recipes a celebrity. ''You sound like Mr. Rafferty. He didn't understand, either. That's why we had the disagreement.''

''Aw, Mom. I thought you really liked him. He's nice, and he's kind of cute for an older guy.''

Carole smiled despite her pain. ''He's not that old.'' He was, however, drop-dead handsome. Sexy as sin. And completely dedicated to his company, not to her. He'd even investigated her behind her back. When she thought of how she'd immersed herself in him for those days…and all the while he wanted to convince her to become Huntington's spokesperson.

''He's 'daddy old,' not 'granddaddy old,''' Jenny explained.

Carole walked into the kitchen, reaching for the scrapbook that she hadn't put away yet. ''Speaking of daddies, why didn't you tell me you'd started collecting pictures of your father?''

Jenny looked down at her pink sneakers. ''Oh, that.''

''It's okay that you wanted to see what he looked like, but I think we should talk about this.''

''Well, you didn't have any pictures, and I had them for everyone else. All my friends have pictures of both their parents, so I thought I'd just cut them out of the magazines.''

''Jenny, you know I haven't talked to your father in ten years. We never had anything to talk about.''

''I know,'' she said in a little voice, ''but that was

a long time ago, before I was even born. What if he wanted to talk now?''

"If he wanted to talk, sweetie," Carole said gently, placing her hands on her daughter's shoulders, "he knows where we live."

Jenny shrugged, which broke Carole's heart. She wanted her father to at least acknowledge her. "I'm sorry, Jenny. Your father and I were very, very young when we got married. He wasn't ready to be a daddy. He's still not ready. He hasn't gotten married again, has he?''

"No."

"See? This is just about him. It has nothing to do with you."

"I'd like to meet him sometime, though. You know, just to say hello."

"I know," Carole said, pulling her daughter close and holding her tight. "I'm sorry he's not ready to be your daddy, but everyone here loves you very much. You're the best part of our family."

"I am?" Jenny asked, looking up. "Better than Aunt Princess Kerry?''

"Absolutely," Carole said, finally feeling like a genuine smile. Ever since Kerry had married Prince Alexi last fall, Jenny had insisted on using both her aunt's titles.

After hugging for just a moment, Jenny pulled away to reach for the plate of cookies. She selected one, then looked up, all casual innocence. "So maybe you should call Mr. Rafferty and see if he left already. Maybe you should ask him to come back and see us."

Carole felt her smile fade. Just like Johnny Ray French, just like her father, Greg Rafferty knew where to find her if he wanted to get in touch. And besides, why should she get in touch when she was the one who was hurt by his single-minded dedication to his idea for saving the company?

GREG WENT to the Four Square Café for lunch on Saturday for the last time. He'd called for the jet to pick him up later today at the regional airport, but he wanted to say goodbye to people he'd met and liked in Ranger Springs.

"Hello, Greg," Mrs. Jacks greeted him, her normally bubbly personality subdued as she grabbed rolled silverware and a menu.

"Good afternoon, Mrs. Jacks. How are you?"

"I'm fine." She placed the menu on top of one of those scenic placemats the café used. "I'm doing a lot better than some people."

"Is she…okay? Did Jennifer get home from camp?"

"No, she's not okay, and yes, Jennifer is home." She put the silverware, wrapped in a paper napkin, down with controlled force. "I'll get you some iced tea."

Maybe this was a mistake. He noticed Thelma Rogers from the paper sitting with her friend Joyce Wheatley and Joyce's husband, Ambrose, who was a semi-retired physician. They weren't glaring at him, but they didn't look real friendly, either. By the front window, the pretty, honey-blond lady who was married to the police chief read her menu, although she probably knew it by heart since her antiques store was right across the square. There were some other folks, but he didn't know them by name or profession.

Mrs. Jacks returned with his tea. "What can I get you?"

"I suppose another chance to talk to Carole is out of the question."

"And definitely not on the menu. That's not something I can give you, Greg. You'll have to find your own way to talk to her."

"She made herself pretty clear. She doesn't trust me and she doesn't want to talk to me again."

"Maybe that's because you keep asking her the same question."

"I only did what I thought was best for both her and my company."

"Seems kind of convenient that your solution is the best thing for both of you, doesn't it?" she said, placing a hand on her hip and giving him a hard, assessing look. "Now, what would you like to eat?"

In honor of his last day in Texas, he ordered the unofficial state meal: chicken-fried steak, mashed potatoes and gravy, Texas toast and a salad with ranch dressing. He doubted he'd be able to eat much since his appetite had deserted him, replaced by an empty gnawing hunger for his beautiful blond cowgirl.

He'd nearly finished when Thelma, Joyce and Ambrose stopped by his table.

"That was a nice thing to do, giving Puff back to Jennifer with an unlimited supply of food," Joyce said. At Greg's raised eyebrow, she continued. "My nephew Lester told me what you'd done. I'm sure Jennifer is going to be thrilled."

"I'm not sure if Carole appreciates the gesture," Greg said, pushing his plate away. He smiled when he remembered his second—or was it his third?—argument with Carole on the first day they'd met. He'd told her he wanted to give the steer back to Jennifer and she'd told him she didn't want him back.

Puff wasn't the only thing she didn't want from him. She didn't want his job offer, his advice, his insights on her parenting or even his...affection. She didn't trust him. She didn't believe him when he swore their brief affair had nothing to do with his desire to convince her to be Huntington's spokesperson.

"Carole can be a little stubborn," Thelma said.

"Ever since that unfortunate incident when she was a teenager," Joyce added.

"Now, honey, don't start telling tales."

Greg ignored the older man, hoping the ladies would keep talking. "I know about her running off and getting married. I even know that the boy she ran off with is now a successful country-western singer. I just still don't understand why people call it an 'unfortunate incident.'"

"Oh, it was just terrible for her. I suppose I can explain since you already know the rest. You see, a film crew did a documentary on the band her husband was in, back before he went solo and got famous. It showed them partying with groupies, taking some drugs and acting like complete idiots. He and Carole had only been married a few weeks and she was just mortified."

"I can only imagine." Had Carole been averse to publicity back then, or had the experience caused her to hate being in the spotlight?

"Fortunately, Charlene saw the documentary as soon as it aired. Poor Carole was too embarrassed to tell her mother what had happened or even where she was. Charlene jumped in the family station wagon and drove to Nashville, since that's where the band was. She brought Carole back here to Rangers Springs and she's been here ever since."

Greg nodded. "So the whole fiasco—Carole running off to get married, the jerk of a husband, the documentary—that was all part of this unfortunate incident."

"That's right," Ambrose said. "Everyone makes mistakes. Carole has grown up to be a fine young woman and a great mother."

"Yes, she is."

"She'd make some man a fine wife," Joyce said wistfully.

Greg was saved from a reply when Charlene Jacks returned to bus the table and present his check. "Anything else?" she asked, looking pointedly from friend to friend.

"No, I think I have everything I came here for."

"I hope you can come back and see us," Thelma said. "I never did get that in-depth interview."

Greg attempted a smile, even though his mind was already skipping ahead. Coming back? He couldn't imagine why at the moment, not when Carole wouldn't talk to him, even to say goodbye. "Maybe later."

Joyce, Thelma and Ambrose wandered off, stopping to talk to Hank McCauley and his wife Gwendolyn, along with Travis Whittaker, who'd just come through the door. Would Carole eventually find a husband in her single neighbor? He seemed to be a nice guy, and Greg assumed women found his blond hair and athletic body attractive.

"I want you to think about what I said," Mrs. Jacks said, bringing his attention back to the table. "About what you really want. Personally, I think you've convinced yourself that what's best for Huntington is also best for Carole. But maybe I'm wrong. And that's all I'm going to say on the subject.''

She stacked the dishes and started to leave, then turned back to face him. ''Except for one more thing. My daughter deserves someone who appreciates her for who she is now. At the same time, it doesn't hurt to give Carole a nudge now and then. It would take a hell of a man to do both.''

Greg nodded his agreement. It would take a hell of a man. Unfortunately, he was first and foremost a C.E.O.

CAROLE INSISTED Jenny take a nap, even though her daughter claimed to be way past the age where sleeping in the afternoon was necessary. Still, she yawned her way to the bedroom and allowed her mother to tuck her in.

Carole walked slowly into the living room, then curled on the couch, staring at the phone. She'd done a lot of thinking while doing laundry. Washing and drying clothes was almost as therapeutic as baking cookies.

Jenny had said something that disturbed her, mainly because Greg had told her the same thing.

Why wouldn't she want to be famous?

She tried really hard to forget her previous disastrous experience with a little bit of fame. If she'd never run away with Johnny Ray, if he hadn't been such a jerk, if the filmmakers hadn't made that documentary for television...if, if, if. She had a lot to forget.

But...if she had graduated from high school with her class, lived happily in the bosom of her family, maybe gone to college like Kerry or married somebody nice like Hank, she would have loved to become famous.

She closed her eyes and visualized her smiling image on a package of Ms. Carole's cookies. Maybe not a photo, but a drawn image. Not a caricature, but more like a line drawing or a simple sketch. Her image on dozens of packages of cookies on grocery shelves around the country.

Then she saw herself sitting in a chair, smiling into a camera, a display of her cookies on the low table in front of herself and the host. Or hostess. Yes, a woman. One whose stylish suit matched her own designer clothing. Perhaps a simple sheath with one nice piece of jewelry, like a pin. Something that said, ''This woman has class.'' She would cross her legs—she'd be wearing really nice hosiery—and show her pointed-toe pumps. Her legs would look great, without any shaving nicks or bruises.

Greg running his hand up her leg, beneath the hem of that stylish sheath.

Her eyes snapped open. So much for visualization. She wasn't supposed to be thinking about *him,* but rather finding who she would have been without her mistakes. And from what she'd imagined, she supposed she would have enjoyed being famous.

But still, she had Jenny to consider. Despite the fact her daughter thought it would be ''neat'' to have a celebrity mother, Carole knew there were drawbacks neither of them could imagine. And what she could imagine frightened her.

She would love the nice conversation and interviews, but what about criticism? She'd never been good at disapproval. What if people really didn't like her?

What did she do now if people didn't like her? She frowned as she tried to think of someone who had been rude or critical, but she couldn't think of anyone in the past several years. Perhaps not since she'd been an adult. She wanted to say that was because she didn't meet new people, but that wasn't true. She gave selected baking demonstrations in Austin and San Antonio, talking to all types of people at some of the exclusive housewares stores. She shopped and did just about everything any other normal mother did. And everyone was polite, most of them nice.

What if the media people were nice, too? What if she was just using her fear of infamy as an excuse to stay nice and safe, never stretching her wings, never taking another chance?

She placed a hand on her stomach as her nerves zinged and her mind raced. Had she really been running that scared? Was Greg right about her fears? She leaned back against the couch, trying to think through all the perceptions these revelations might shatter.

And most of all, what if Johnny Ray still didn't want to be a father and didn't do one darned thing if the public found out he'd briefly been married to the cookie queen of Ranger Springs?

Before she lost her nerve to face these what-ifs, she picked up the phone and called her sister Kerry's private number in Belegovia. Their mother was right; if anyone could tell her what it was like to face public criticism and adoration, Princess Kerry, the former truck-stop waitress who'd run off with a prince, was the one.

Chapter Fifteen

Greg packed up the last of his clothes, tugging the zipper closed over his Western shirts, jeans and blister-producing boots. He'd been tempted to leave the clothes behind, but he'd gotten rather attached to them.

He might not be leaving his physical belongings in Texas, but he felt as though he was leaving his heart. Or what heart he had. He supposed most of his feelings were tied up with Huntington Foods, but what he had left, he'd given to Carole, Jenny and a twelve-hundred-pound steer.

He slung the bag over his shoulder and headed for the door. The plane should be landing right about now. In a few hours he'd be back in Chicago, preparing for the board meeting on Monday. Except, he had too much time. An entire day to kill, with nothing to think about but how he'd screwed up his relationship with Carole.

The phone rang, stopping him halfway out the door. His pulse began to race. Not many people would know to call him at the house. His business associates and family would use the cell.

He dropped the bag and reached for the wall phone. "Hello?"

Only a faint sound of breathing greeted him. Then the voice he'd longed to hear again. "Greg?"

"Carole." He breathed her name with a sigh of relief. "I wanted to call you, but I didn't think you'd want to talk to me."

"I didn't call to chat."

"No, of course not. Are you okay?"

"I'm fine."

And her tone of voice said that she wanted to keep this conversation light. Calling must have been difficult for her. After all, he didn't have the guts to dial her number.

"I'm glad you called," he finally said.

She sighed. "I was afraid you might have already gone back to Chicago."

"I was just on my way to the airport," he said, then added quickly, "but I'm not in any hurry. The plane will wait."

"I...I've been thinking about what you offered."

Greg pulled out a kitchen chair and sat down before his legs failed him. "Offered?"

"About the spokesperson position."

"Oh." Why did he feel let down when this is what he'd wanted all along? What he'd come to Texas to accomplish? "Of course. You've perhaps changed your mind?"

"Maybe you had a point when you said I was scared. I got to thinking, after I talked to Jenny, that maybe I was focusing too much on the negative and not letting myself go after something that might be good for all of us."

"We'd certainly like to make it worth your while," he said, slipping into his business mode with more difficulty than usual. "And I promise we'll do everything we can to ensure those negatives possibilities don't become reality.''

"I talked to my sister. She said no one can plan for all possibilities.''

"No, but we have many resources, many people, who can think about different scenarios. We also have a legal department than can help with those problems.'' Greg paused, then asked, "Did you sister have any good things to say?''

He almost heard Carole smile. "She said the clothes and shoes alone were almost worth the trouble.''

Greg chuckled, then fell silent, unsure what to say next. He didn't want to pressure Carole. And she remained silent for so long he almost made some inane comment.

But then she asked, "So, what do we do now?''

"I don't suppose you want to go back to Chicago with me on the jet.''

"No, I have a napping daughter who just got back from camp,'' she said with enough exasperation to let him know he'd asked the wrong question. "I'm not going to completely change my life. I'm not going to sacrifice my daughter's life for financial gain and celebrity status, but I'm willing to compromise on the details of scheduling appearances and making commercials.''

"I understand.'' He paused, twisting the phone cord. "What about us?''

"All I'm talking about is the spokesperson job. I'm not prepared for anything else. I can't handle anything else, not when I can't completely trust you, Greg. I can't be sure you didn't use our relationship to influence me.''

"I didn't, although there's no way to prove it.''

"Perhaps it's best this way. We rushed into a…an affair based on strong chemistry. That's not a good basis for anything beyond a short fling."

At least she didn't say she wasn't interested. Or that she wouldn't consider a personal relationship. So maybe there was some hope, if he handled this correctly. Carefully. "When can you come to Chicago? I'll set up appointments with our public relations department and a stylist who'll help you prepare for some sample tapings."

"This is happening so fast."

"We need you Carole." *I need you,* he wanted to say, but knew his company came first, for him and, at the moment, for her. He sure didn't want to scare her off by confusing the issue. She had to know that Huntington was a separate deal from anything he might have to offer. Not that he was offering. They'd both known their personal relationship was temporary.

"I could probably get my sister Cheryl and my mother to watch Jenny next week."

"I'd say bring her with you, but you'll be really busy. Booked pretty heavy." Too busy to have time for him, that's for sure. He'd make sure of that.

"I'd rather keep her away from this for as long as possible. Besides, she's starting school on Wednesday."

"Whatever you'd like. Of course, I'd always enjoy having her visit Huntington."

"Yes, Huntington. Of course. Well, I'll tell her. She…she asked about you. She wanted to say goodbye."

He dropped the twisted cord and leaned forward between his bent knees. "Did she have a good time at camp?"

"Yes," Carole answered with a smile in her voice, "if you consider snakes, swimming and friends overdosing on cupcakes fun."

Greg smiled, thinking about Jennifer giving a blow-by-blow of camp life. "Tell her I said hello, and that I'll see her again as soon as possible. And remind her to take good care of my steer."

"I'll tell her."

Greg paused, tempted to drop the phone, drive to Carole's house, and take her into his arms. He took a deep breath. "So, how about Tuesday? I'll send the jet."

Her nervous laugh answered him. "Okay. Tuesday, then. And how long should I plan to be in Chicago?"

"Can you give me four days?" He closed his eyes. What a stupid way to phrase the question. He should have said *us*. He should have asked if she could stay in Chicago four days.

"Three."

"Done. I'll see you on Tuesday."

She hung up the phone as soon as he said goodbye. Greg sat in the kitchen of his rented house and wondered just how much his life would be changing in the next weeks or months. How could he work with Carole and not remember the taste of her skin or the feel of her lips, moving against his?

He couldn't. He'd have to keep a firm grip on his emotions, because he would not let his feelings frighten away the perfect spokesperson for his company.

DURING THE NEXT TWO WEEKS Carole flew to Chicago three times, each visit a whirlwind of appointments, meetings and rehearsals. She'd declined extra highlights in her hair, although she'd gotten a good trim at an overpriced salon. She had a new professional wardrobe, tailored to her exact measurements, and had finally gotten accustomed to her new manicure, pedicure and makeup.

Kerry was right; the new clothes and shoes were almost worth the inconvenience of becoming famous. Not that the cookie queen of Ranger Springs would ever be as popular as a real princess of a foreign country.

When she looked into the mirror, she was the same, yet different. She was Carole Jacks, but also Ms. Carole. She was still Jennifer's mother, but also a professional woman whose image would, hopefully, become recognizable to thousands, if not millions, of consumers.

Greg often looked at her with unreadable eyes. Sometimes she felt as though he was trying very hard not to react to her new appearance, but that was probably wishful thinking. Not that she wanted to continue their affair, but she would like to know that he was suffering just a little. That he felt almost as frustrated and sad as she sometimes did when she remembered their days together back in Texas.

But she couldn't think about that now. She had to concentrate on the commercial they were taping at the studio not too far from Huntington's offices in downtown Chicago. She'd tried not to think of Greg often, especially at night, alone in her hotel room. She longed for her mother, her sisters and her daughter. But they were far away, and Greg was nearby. And, Lord help her, she still wanted him.

She apparently hadn't learned her lessons regarding men. She had lousy taste. She made bad choices.

Hopefully, she'd keep that in mind whenever she felt tempted to let her emotions rule her body.

"Ms. Carole, we're ready for you," the director of the commercial announced.

"Knock 'em dead," Greg's mother advised, smiling as she looked across the top of her stylish half glasses. Over the past several weeks, Carole had grown to depend on Roberta Rafferty's advice and encouragement. Greg's mother was a true professional woman. She wasn't the warm and fuzzy type, but she knew the business world into which Carole had been thrust. She trusted Roberta's advice as much as she doubted Greg's motives.

He'd respected her wishes, not discussing their brief affair, but she would have preferred a more forceful denial that he'd seduced her just to get her cooperation. Okay, he hadn't really seduced her; she'd gone to him. But that was beside the point. He was the one with the experience, the skill, and he'd known exactly what he was doing.

Whereas she had fumbled around like a silly buckle bunny with a severe crush on the best bronc rider in the arena.

"Carole? We're waiting for you to take your seat."

She took a deep breath. "Right." Forcing a smile at the director, she marched toward the lights, camera and action.

THE FIRST COMMERCIAL featuring the real Ms. Carole would air during the afternoon talk shows, and Greg felt a growing sense of excitement as company officials, his family and Carole herself gathered in the conference room. She looked tense to him, but he was sure few people picked up on her nervous energy. She sipped coffee as she made the circuit of the room, moving ever closer to the door.

He moved to intercept her before she slipped outside.

"Going somewhere?" he asked.

"The ladies' room." She appeared even more tense. In fact, she looked a little green. She'd done a live radio interview earlier for one of the syndicates around the country, and although she'd handled the questions beautifully, she was probably a mass of nerves.

"I'll go with you."

She started to protest, but hurried away instead. Greg waited in the hallway, nodding to Huntington employees as he waited for Carole. Just as he was about to violate the sanctity of the women's rest room, she walked out.

"Better?"

She nodded. "I just needed a minute to myself...and a wet paper towel. I'm not that sick...unless I start thinking about myself on national television."

Greg glanced at his watch. "It's almost time. Do you feel up to going back in to see your commercial?"

"I don't know. I'm so nervous."

"I know, but you've seen it before. This is just a ceremonial event for us. We're all very proud of you, Carole. Mother, especially, is thrilled with the campaign."

She looked down at her stylish red high-heeled sandals. "There were times when I didn't think I could do this."

"But you did. The worst part is over, in my opinion. Now you can go around the country and do interviews, but you have the skills and the wardrobe."

"I'm still not too keen on flying to various cities."

"I know, but we haven't scheduled very many, and besides, the corporate jet makes it a lot more convenient."

Carole nodded. "I'll be able to take Jenny with me during some of her school breaks or weekends."

"She'll like that." He gazed at his own shoes, seeing dusty cowboy boots in his mind. "How is she?" He missed the ten-year-old, which he could never have imagined. He even missed Puff, Mrs. Jacks and some of the café regulars. He'd only had contact with Thelma Rogers, whom he'd called to give that long-awaited interview. He figured the local publicity would be good for Carole and explain their relationship to those who speculated about his time in Ranger Springs.

"She's fine. She misses me," Carole said as they started walking back to the conference room. "She asks about you every time we talk."

"Maybe she should come to Chicago next time."

"I'm trying not to disrupt her life."

Greg stopped her with a hand on her elbow. She turned, a question in her eyes. Was that also longing he saw? Or perhaps his imagination put an emotion into the equation that no longer existed.

"Did I disrupt your life too much, Carole?"

She looked up at him. Yes, he saw longing. His heart raced as she answered. "No, not too much. I needed this. I needed to shake up my world or I would have become a reclusive, overprotective mother who spent her entire life baking for her small community, talking to the same people, shopping in the same stores."

"Still, that can be a good life."

"But now Jenny's college will be paid for, the

house will be paid off and I have enough for a rainy day.''

She glanced toward the conference room door. "I guess we should go in."

"Yes." He looked down the hallway at the corporate offices of the company he loved. "I used to visit my grandfather in these offices. Even when I was a child, I wanted to be the boss. I'm telling you this because I want you to understand how important it is to me to save the reputation of Huntington Foods."

"I know it's important to you. That was never my problem with your...pursuit of my cooperation. I just didn't agree with—"

"Hey, you guys, it's almost time," Stephanie called from the conference room. "You'd better get in here."

"Let's continue this conversation later," Greg suggested. "Can I pick you up at your hotel for dinner?"

Carole took a deep breath, molding the knit fabric of her dress over those perfect breasts. He wanted her now more than ever. Time hadn't dimmed his desire. Distance from the heat of cowboy country hadn't cooled his passion.

"What time?" she asked.

INSTEAD OF TRYING to impress her with big-city wealth, Greg chose a family-owned restaurant not far from his condo. They dined on Italian food—the urban equivalent of Tex-Mex, Greg claimed—and then walked side by side to the car.

Walking hand in hand would have felt right, Carole realized as they approached Greg's sporty BMW. She wondered if he sensed the attraction, too, or if she was the only one with lust in her heart.

Or maybe it wasn't lust. Maybe it was something

more. Maybe she'd fallen in love with Greg Rafferty sometime between him buying Puff and her watching the pride on his face when the commercial played during a break in *Oprah* today.

"Would you like to come up to my place and talk?" he asked as they reached the car.

"I suppose." *Yes!* She wanted to be alone with him, to see if what she felt was some sort of residual from today's excitement or a culmination of all the time they'd spent together in Texas and Chicago.

The drive was less than a mile, but took a lot longer than a mile in Ranger Springs due to the heavy city traffic. Carole grew more and more tense in the silence of the interior. Why didn't Greg say something witty?

He parked in the garage and she followed him to the elevator, her steps beginning to drag. Was she making a mistake? She began to feel the way she had before they'd made love the first time—insecure and indecisive.

The small elevator finally opened and she stepped inside the fake wood and brushed-metal interior. Greg's expression was unreadable. He hit the button to the twenty-second floor, the doors closed, and he turned to her.

Oh, Lord. His eyes burned bright with passion. He framed her face with his hands seconds before his mouth crushed down on hers, before he pushed her back against the faux wood wall.

He kissed her until her head swam and her knees sagged. His hard chest flattened her breasts as his arousal pressed against her stomach. She moved against him, her passion rising more quickly than the elevator. He tasted of rich spices and smelled so familiar her heart ached.

They barely made it into the apartment. She wondered if she'd jump the gun the way she did the first time. Fortunately, during her days with Greg back in Ranger Springs, she'd learned not to worry about having too many climaxes.

He started to carry her toward his bedroom, but then stopped in the darkened hallway, pressing her against the wall, his hands once again framing her face. "Carole," he whispered, his breathing ragged, "I know I said I wanted to talk, but I want to make love to you more. I've missed you so much."

"I've missed you, too. I tried not to, but I couldn't help myself, even when I wasn't sure of your motives."

"I've always been honest with you. I didn't buy Puff to impress you. I didn't seduce you to make you vulnerable to my arguments. I didn't fall in love with you to make you become our spokesperson. My feelings have nothing—"

"Wait," she said, placing her fingers against his warm, firm lips. "What did you say?"

"I said I've fallen in love with you." He kissed her again, this time slow and gentle. "I love you, Carole."

"Oh, Greg, I love you, too. I really do." She slid her arms around his neck and held on tight. "And I trust you. I know you were honest with me. I didn't before, but now I realize you were always truthful. You wouldn't do anything to hurt me."

"Never."

"Make love to me, Greg."

He wrapped his arms around her to carry her into the bedroom, and this time she wrapped her legs around him and held on tight. When they undressed in the low light coming from the bathroom, Carole felt no trepidation about her body, her stretch marks or her ability to satisfy him. Overwhelmed with love, she gave herself completely, and in return, received his love with an open heart.

Afterward, they lay together, reality slowly returning. There would be schedules to coordinate, details to discuss, but she believed they could negotiate anything now that they'd revealed their love. Jenny already adored Greg, and he seemed genuinely fond of her also. Yes, everything would be fine now. She'd finally made the right decision regarding a man, regarding her future.

CAROLE'S OPTIMISM lasted through the night spent in Greg's arms, a breakfast of croissants and strawberries eaten half-dressed in bed, and the drive back to the hotel for her to get more clothes and toiletries. She'd accepted his plan for her to stay at his condo until she left for Texas tomorrow. Every minute together felt precious. She couldn't wait for him to return to Ranger Springs so they could talk about the details of their relationship. Their future.

Giggling because he couldn't keep his hands off her, she finally managed to unlock her hotel room door and stumble inside. She felt giddy, as though they'd had a magnum of champagne with their breakfast instead of orange juice and coffee.

She put her index finger to her lips and signaled him to be quiet as she sat behind the desk and hit the message button on the phone with the blinking red light. As she impatiently worked her way through the voice mail system, she watched Greg lounge in the wing-back chair in the corner of the room. He appeared to be every woman's dream, one hundred percent virile male. Only she knew his other attributes: patience, intelligence, persistence and imagination.

Her smile faded as she listened to a message from her mother. A frantic message that chilled Carole's blood.

"Johnny Ray's manager called from Los Angeles. Someone who knew you'd once been married heard your radio interview and told him about you now being a celebrity. His manager said that Johnny isn't going to let you say anything negative about him, like the fact you got your marriage annulled and that he's never seen his daughter. Carole, he threatened all kinds of legal problems if you mention Johnny Ray. I've been trying to reach you, and I'm so scared you're going to say or do something to make him angry. Please, please call me. I'm keeping all this from Jennifer—for now. Call me. 'Bye.''

Carole felt the blood roar in her ears as it drained from her face. She dropped the phone onto the desk and stared unseeing at the bed.

"Carole, what's wrong?"

She vaguely felt Greg's hands on her arms as she lifted her head to stare at him. "It's my nightmare."

"What? Tell me, sweetheart."

"Johnny Ray knows I'm going to be your new spokesperson. He's threatening me with legal action, Greg. He thinks I'm trying to make him look bad, since he doesn't know his own daughter."

"We'll get our lawyers on this, Carole. Everything will be fine. He's not going to hurt you."

"Me? Is that what you think this is about?" She shook her head, tears blurring her vision. "He can't really hurt me, but he can destroy Jenny's dreams. I tried so hard to make sure she didn't miss having a father in her life, and now he's going to hurt her forever just because I wanted everyone to know that I'm Ms. Carole...that those are my cookie recipes they're enjoying.'' She turned her face into Greg's chest and sobbed, ''What have I done to my baby?''

Chapter Sixteen

"Remember not to say anything, even to your friends. We'll let the professionals handle this, okay?"

"Then where are you going? I really need you here," Carole said, holding him tight in the small waiting room of the regional airport where the corporate jet landed.

"I'll be back tomorrow at the latest. Earlier if I can." He rested his chin on her head. "This is something I have to do, sweetheart. Something I can't avoid."

"Just hurry back. Even though Jenny doesn't know anything about what Johnny Ray said, she may sense something is wrong. And she could hear us talking."

"Just be careful about what you say, and I'll be back before you know it."

She pulled back, her expression so sad it almost broke his heart. "I should have stayed in Ranger Springs. I never should have thought I could pull this off without problems."

"That's not true!" His hands tightened on her upper arms, but he forced himself to be calm. "This is not your fault."

"It sure feels like it," she said, closing her eyes and

looking out the windows to the small parking lot. "I'd better go. Cheryl is waiting for me."

"I'll be back before you know it, and then we'll talk."

Carole nodded and stepped out of his embrace. "Have a safe trip."

"I love you, Carole."

She hugged her arms around herself and nodded, as though she didn't trust herself to speak. He'd take that explanation with him, rather than the one that said she no longer loved him. That she'd spoken in a moment of passion and now realized her feelings weren't genuine.

He turned and hurried through the heat shimmering off the pavement toward the jet, which had been refueled and checked out for the flight west.

To Los Angeles. To speak man-to-man to Johnny Ray French and his attorneys. Because unlike his advice to Carole, he wasn't going to be quiet about this. He wasn't going to let the lawyers handle it. He was the Huntington C.E.O. *and* the man in love with Ms. Carole; how could he do anything else when his future depended on success?

CAROLE GATHERED her family and friends around her like a security blanket, insisting on a big meal at her house tonight even though she'd barely gotten into town by two o'clock this afternoon. They'd suggested potluck, so she'd immersed herself in cake batter and cookie dough, and Jenny told stories over little bottles of bright-colored sprinkles and bowls of chocolate chips.

My daughter is fine, she kept telling herself as she scooped out the last batch onto a cookie sheet. She

knows nothing of her father's legal threats and she
didn't need to know. Greg's corporate attorneys would
get this mess straightened out in the time it took her
to clean up this messy kitchen.

"Last batch in," she announced with a big smile.
"I'll set the timer and then you can help me load the
dishwasher."

"Aw, Mom."

Carole smiled again, this time genuine. "I'm gone
for days and you complain about spending time with
me."

"How about we blast some space aliens on my new
game machine?" Jenny offered. "That's more fun
than dishes."

"I want the kitchen to be all clean for our dinner
tonight. Aunt Cheryl and Grandma and Uncle Hank
and Gwendolyn and lots of people are coming over."

"I know. Okay, I'll help." Jenny grabbed the big
mixing bowl and carried it to the sink. "Why don't
you tell me what you did in Chicago this time?"

I bared my heart to the man I love, Carole felt like
saying. Later, maybe she could talk to her mother. Oh,
she wished her older sister was here. Kerry always
gave great advice, but she was thousands of miles
away in Belegovia, no doubt attending some fancy
dinner instead of a pot luck supper.

"There was a little party at the Huntington Foods
office when my first commercial aired during *Oprah*.
That was kind of neat, but I got really nervous and
almost threw up lunch."

"Gross," Jenny said with a smile. "So did they
serve Ms. Carole's cookies?"

She laughed. "Yes, but they also had a really pretty
cake with fresh berries and white chocolate roses, and

we drank champagne and everyone was happy." *And then I went out to dinner with Greg, and we made love and then I confirmed that your father is a self-centered jerk.*

"Neat."

They finished cleaning the kitchen, then went outside and fed Puff his dinner. The big steer was even more a baby now than when Jenny had shown him. Carole wondered what in the world they would eventually do with the animal, since he could easily live another twenty years.

By the time Puff died, Jenny would be grown and married. Carole would probably be a grandmother, or might be in a few years. And what about Greg? Would he be in the picture twenty years from now, or would he be just a memory?

She shook away the depressing thoughts. She needed to stay busy.

"Let's go back inside and set the buffet. Our guests will be here before we know it."

"More work," Jenny groused, but she put Puff's brush in the bucket inside the tack room, grabbed Carole's hand and together they walked into the house.

Company was scheduled for six o'clock. At five thirty-five Carole heard gravel crunch on the driveway. She hurried to the front door, expecting to see her mother and sister, but instead, a familiar black Land Rover pulled to a stop. Pete Boedecker stepped out of the driver's side, waved, then went to the rear door. A stern, dark-suited, large man who looked as if he could snap a telephone pole in two exited, looked around and nodded. Within a second Kerry bounded out of the back seat. Or as much as she could bound while holding a squirming six-month-old prince.

"Hey, big sister," Carole yelled, rushing down the steps.

Kerry handed her baby to the big guy, who'd been joined by an equally imposing man in a dark suit, and held her arms out to Carole. "It's so good to see you."

"I'm so glad you're here," Carole said, pulling back. "I didn't know how much I needed to talk to you until this afternoon. It's like you read my mind."

"No, I just listened to Mom. What she said and what she didn't say. You, little sister, have problems."

Carole felt her lip tremble as if she were still a child. "You're right, I do. And I don't know what to do about it."

"Aunt Princess Kerry!" Jenny squealed, running down the steps.

They all hugged, then went into the house with the very healthy and vocal Prince Alexander. He hadn't liked being confined in his car seat and wanted everyone to know about it. Fortunately, Jenny offered to take him into the newly cleaned kitchen, where he could crawl around on the floor to his heart's content.

"So, what happened with Johnny Ray? Mom told me the story."

"I don't know yet. Greg said we should let the lawyers handle it."

"Greg?"

"Mama didn't tell you?"

"No, she left out that juicy morsel."

"I'm shocked." Carole took a deep breath. "He's the C.E.O. of Huntington Foods and he came down here to ask me to be the new spokesperson for the company."

"Wow. The real Ms. Carole. Finally."

"You just assumed I said yes."

"Mom told me you were in Chicago taping commercials. I made a giant leap. So, tell me about Greg."

She looked into the kitchen and saw Jenny on the floor, rolling a ball to the future king of Belegovia. Carole leaned forward and said in a low voice, "He's...I'm in love with him...I think."

"You think?"

"I knew I was in love with him in Chicago," she whispered, "but then I got a message from Mama about Johnny Ray, and I knew I'd made a big mistake. Again. I knew I shouldn't be there in Chicago, all dressed up as Ms. Carole, giving interviews and smiling into cameras. What do I know about publicity? For that matter, what do I know about *men?*"

"Shh," Kerry said. "Answer this. Why do you love Greg?"

Carole leaned back in her chair and frowned. "This all happened so fast. I don't know how to answer that question."

"Right now, do you feel like you love him?"

"I don't know. I think I do, but then everything else comes into my mind. My poor decisions in the past. My roots in small town Texas. Greg says he loves me and I believe him, but I'm not sure I can do this."

"Do what, sweetie?"

"Be the love of his life. Be the savior of his company's reputation. Be the best mother I can be to my daughter, who has a big jerk for a biological father." She shook her head. "Sometimes it's too much, Kerry."

Kerry moved to sit on the side of the chair and put her arm around her little sister. The same sister who had caused so much family grief at the time Kerry was graduating from high school and worrying about how she was going to pay for college.

"It's okay. We all feel that way. You just have a few more issues, that's all. And this is all new to you. All this relationship angst and self-doubt. You've been so mature and competent for so long that you aren't used to being insecure about yourself as a woman or a mother."

"Until I met Greg, I didn't know what it meant to be a woman."

"Ah, so it's like that. Well, good for you."

Carole frowned. "Why do you say that?"

"Because now you know what the rest of us who are in love know. It's not always easy. It's often not convenient. Lord knows, falling in love with a prince in four days wasn't exactly on my agenda while I was graduating from college. Getting pregnant when I'd just started a new job wasn't a good idea. But hey, those things happen. And you know what? I wouldn't change a thing. I love Alexi with all my heart."

"Do you ever wish you could just turn back the clock? That you weren't in the truck stop when he came in?"

"No. Never." Kerry took her hand. "Do you ever wish Greg hadn't sought you out to represent his company? Do you wish you hadn't gotten involved with him?"

Carole sat back in her chair and gazed into the wise, beautiful face of her big sister. And just then the door burst open and all her guests arrived, potluck dishes in hand.

CAROLE'S GUESTS were just finishing seconds of her mother's coconut layer cake and Gwendolyn's strawberry trifle when there was a knock at the door. Kerry and Alex's two unobtrusive bodyguards, who had been eating in the living room rather than around the crowded table, answered it with stern faces before the family could respond.

Carole heard the hum of men's voices, but she couldn't see beyond the men's broad backs into the dusk. She felt drawn, though, as if someone was calling her. Someone who shouldn't be here until tomorrow.

"Greg?" she said softly as she skirted the hulks and looked outside.

"Carole," he said softly, "would you tell these gentlemen that it's okay for me to come in?"

"Of course. This is Greg Rafferty, C.E.O. of Huntington Foods. He's…expected."

Carole stepped back with a tentative smile. Greg's expression, as was so often the case, was unreadable, yet intense. He stepped into her small foyer off the living room, but the door didn't close right away. She saw another man's shape outlined by the porch light, but didn't recognize him. Had Greg brought a guest? A business associate?

"Mr. Rafferty!" Jenny exclaimed, bursting into the room with energy to burn. "I'm so glad you came to our potluck supper. I really missed you. Puff missed you, too."

Greg hunkered down until he was at eye level. "He did? Well, I'll have to give him a special treat when I see him."

"Yeah," her crafty daughter said, "treats are nice."

Greg laughed, but then his smile faded. He stood up, but kept one hand on Jenny's shoulder. He turned to look at the other man, whom Carole had forgotten about while watching the interchange between Greg and Jenny. They looked so darn good together.

Like father and daughter. There. She'd at least internally voiced the words that she dared not speak.

"Carole, Jenny, there's someone here who needs to talk to you."

Someone behind them flipped on the overhead light. Only then did she see who stood inside her home. A collective gasp from her family and friends indicated they'd noticed, too.

"Johnny Ray," she whispered, feeling her legs turn to lime gelatin. "What the…heck are you doing here?"

"Hello there, Carole. You look real good, darlin'." He grinned as though he didn't have a care in the world, then looked down at his daughter. The child he never wanted or acknowledged. "And you must be Jennifer Lynn. Mr. Rafferty told me all about you."

"Daddy?" Jennifer said, holding tight to Carole's side.

"I guess I am at that, but believe me, little darlin', that's a title no one's used on me before."

"Why are you here?" Carole asked, her voice sounding more harsh than she'd intended as she hugged Jenny closer.

"Greg here asked me to come so we could straighten everything out. I hope this isn't a bad time for you."

As if that would really bother him. "No, this is a great time. The whole family is here. Of course, you didn't really get to meet them before. My mother, Charlene Jacks, who drove to Nashville in the family station wagon to bring me home. My older sister, Kerry, who is now a princess, and her son Alexander.

My younger sister, Cheryl, who has often threatened to—well, never mind. And these are my friends, Hank and Gwendolyn McCauley. She's an English lady, by the way, so don't pour on the good-ol'-boy routine too thick."

"No need to be snippy, Carole," he said, slightly peeved.

"No need to be gracious, either, until I find out why you're here."

"I asked him to come," Greg replied, "so we could clear up everything once and for all."

She narrowed her eyes at the man she might just love. "I thought the lawyers were supposed to handle this."

Greg shrugged. "They were too slow. I preferred the more direct route."

"He's a real straight shooter, Carole. You might try keepin' this one."

She glared at her ex-husband. She had to admit he looked good. Of course, he was a big star now. Or at least a star. He wasn't Garth Brooks or George Strait. At some point Johnny must have stopped drinking and smoking dope, because he didn't look like the dissipated slob she'd imagined for years, despite seeing his photo in the magazines when she couldn't avoid it, or hearing his songs on the radio if she didn't turn it off fast enough.

"Carole, we'd best be going so you can talk. Call me in the morning, you hear?" her mother said.

"Do you want me here?" Kerry asked.

"Only if you can loan me your bodyguards for about thirty minutes…later, if needed."

Kerry gave an evil chuckle. "I'll be at the Robin's Nest if you need me, in the shabby chic room. These two," she said, eyeing the stern-faced men, "will be in the cowboy suite." A sleepy baby Alex nestled against her chest as they all departed for the Land Rover.

"Gwendolyn and I are only a stone's throw away if you need us," Hank reminded her, heading for the door.

"Lovely to meet you," Gwendolyn said to Johnny Ray in a frosty voice that implied anything but.

Carole's mother came up and hugged her, then turned to her former son-in-law. "Don't you dare do or say anything to hurt this family or you'll be singing a higher note, you hear me?" Carole had rarely heard her mother use that tone of voice.

"Yes, ma'am," Johnny Ray said, not appearing too chastised. Well, why should he be? He was nearly thirty, rich, famous and good-looking. He probably didn't have a care in the world.

"That goes double for me," Cheryl said, taking their mother's arm.

"Good night, Mama," Carole said as Charlene gave one last glare at Johnny before heading for her car.

Finally all the guests were gone except Greg and Johnny Ray. Jenny still clung to her, uncertain as only a child can be when faced with adult issues.

"Let's have a seat. If you're hungry, go grab some food. My family brought enough for an army."

"Maybe later," Greg said, taking a seat on the couch. Carole sat beside him, but not too close. Jenny sat beside her. Right beside her. Johnny Ray took the big easy chair opposite them.

"Carole, I understand your mother got a call from my manager. I'm real sorry if he upset her. I'll have a talk with him tomorrow."

"Yes, she was upset. Are you telling me that you didn't instruct him to threaten us with legal action?"

Johnny shook his head. "He might have taken it that way, but that's not what I meant." He looked at Jennifer and smiled. "You sure are a pretty girl. You look a lot like your mother, but you've got a little of my coloring, don't you?" He leaned back as if he were studying the situation. "The truth is, Jennifer, that your mama and I got married real young. Too young I had to take her to Arkansas so we could get married right away, without her mama's consent. And I shouldn't have done that. All I can say is that I was young and stupid."

"Why did you do it, then?"

"Ah, darlin', that's a long story and kind of personal between me and your mama. Let's just say I wasn't ready to be a husband or a father."

"Oh."

"Truth is, I never thought about having a kid. Er, a child. I guess I knew I wasn't ready. When your mama said she was going to have a baby, I just didn't know what to do. I freaked out for a while."

"But what about now? I wrote you a letter Uncle Hank helped me mail it. I just wanted you to call me."

Johnny shook his head. "I never got your letter, but I'm sure it was a good one. You see, I have a bunch of people who work for me and do things like sort my mail and just give me the things I'm looking for. And Jenny, I know this doesn't sound very nice, but I wasn't ever lookin' to be a father. I still don't know the first thing about havin' a child. I'm what they call a biological father, not a real daddy."

"You don't want me to be your daughter?" Carole hugged her baby close as she heard the insecurity in

Jenny's voice. The same type of insecurity Carole often saw in herself. She just wanted someone to love her. That's all anyone wanted, she supposed.

"I think you have a great family right here in Ranger Springs. Your mama and your grandmother, your aunts and everyone else. They all love you because they've known you for a long time. Me? I don't have much time to get to know people. I travel a lot and don't see my friends much when I'm on the road. I don't have time for a family."

"Oh. That doesn't sound like it's very fun," Jenny said.

"You might be right, but I sure do like a good audience," Johnny said with a big grin. His smile faded as he leaned forward, his attention focused solely on Jenny. "Now, I'm not much of a father figure, I admit. But I know someone who is. See this man?" he asked, pointing to Greg. "He's a really nice guy and I think he loves you a lot. He'd make a terrific dad. If I were you, I'd get my mama to marry him right away so you could be a real family."

"Marry Greg?" Jenny asked, temporarily distracted by this new concept. "I thought he was a C.E.O. and kept getting you to do things you didn't want to do."

Carole shrugged and forced a smile. "Sometimes. Sometimes he gets me to do things I want to do."

He grinned back. "I have my moments."

"If my mom married you, would you be my dad?"

"If she would do me the honor, I would marry her in a minute and be your daddy forever."

Jenny frowned, looking between Johnny Ray and Greg as Carole's heart raced and blood pounded so loud she didn't think she could hear her daughter speak.

"Er, Jenny, I think I need to discuss something this serious with Mr. Rafferty alone."

"Okay," she said, standing up with the sudden resiliency of youth. "I'll take my biological father out to see Puff."

"No, you won't. It's dark outside and…well, I just don't want you wandering around at night."

"Can I sit in here and talk to him then? You and Mr. Rafferty can go to your room. But don't be gone too long. I want to get this father issue settled right away."

"Jenny! It's not that easy."

"Sure it is, Carole," Johnny Ray advised. "Look, go talk with your boyfriend. I'm not going anywhere. Greg here drove over from the airport. I'll talk to Jennifer, get to know her better. I hear she's got a really nice steer that won county 4-H grand champion."

"Carole?" Greg asked.

"Okay, but neither one of you are going anywhere," she said, giving Jenny the look that usually kept her in line.

Greg took her hand and helped her up from the couch. She led him into the guest bedroom, which she also used as an office, keeping the door open so she could hear a door shut or Jenny make any noise. She still didn't trust Johnny Ray, even though he was being pretty nice. He'd explained the situation to Jenny with a surprising level of sensitivity.

"I haven't had time to prepare for this," Greg said, bringing her attention back to him. Back to them. "I didn't make a side trip to a jewelry store or talk to my attorney or anything. I don't want a prenuptial agreement, nor do I have any preconceived notions about the type of wedding we should have."

He knelt in front of her chair, taking her hands in his. "All I know is that I want to marry you, Carole Lynn Jacks. I want to spend the rest of my life with you and Jenny, and maybe produce a couple of brothers or sisters for her to play with. She'd make a great big sister."

"Yes, she would," Carole said softly, running her fingers over the back of his hand. "And what are we going to do about the fact that your job and your family are in Chicago? Everything I know and love is here in Texas."

"Do you love me?"

"With all my heart."

"Then everything we both love will be with us always, no matter where we are. We can get a house just outside Chicago, someplace big with room to grow. And we can come back to Texas for long weekends and all the holidays, whenever you want. We'll build a bigger house here on your land, if you'd like. Whatever you want, we'll work it out."

"If my sister could compromise on marrying a prince of a foreign country, I think I could learn to live in Chicago—at least part time. As long as I can come back to Texas."

"When I retire from being C.E.O. of Huntington, which might be in another ten years or so, we'll retire down here. I'll learn to be more than a catalog cowboy, and you can bake to your heart's content. How does that sound?"

She thought about it for a minute, then looped her arms around Greg's neck and grinned. "If you think you're going to retire and lie around the house with nothing to do but eat my cookies at the ripe old age of forty-two, you're got another think coming."

"Ms. Carole," Greg drawled, "I'm planning on eating a whole lot of your cookies before, during and after my forty-second birthday. Now give me a kiss and tell me again how much you love me, because I've got to admit, bringing your famous ex-husband home to talk was one of the hardest things I've ever done."

"And one of the nicest. Thank you for giving us the peace of mind we could never have gotten through lawyers."

"You're very welcome. And now, maybe we'd better go back in there before Jenny makes him commit to dedicating his next album to her pet steer."

They walked into the living room, where Jenny and her biological father were going through her scrapbook.

"Good news," Greg announced. "Your plan worked. We're getting married as soon as we can make arrangements."

"A fall wedding right here in Ranger Springs, at Bretford House," Carole said, looking into the eyes of the man she loved. "This time, I want all my family to be there with me. I want the whole world to know."

"Cool," Jenny responded, looking up. "Can Puff be the ring bearer? After all, he's the one who got you guys together in the first place."

"We'll talk about it," Greg said.

"That's a very father-like answer," Jenny replied, grinning, running over to give him a hug.

Carole felt joy bubble up inside her as she laughed and hugged both of the people she loved best in the world—and completely forgot about her famous ex-husband, sitting all alone at the table with nothing but photos. He might have money and fame, but she had everything that was important, right here in her arms.

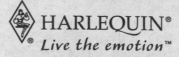

An offer you can't afford to refuse!

High-valued coupons for upcoming books

A sneak peek at Harlequin's newest line—Harlequin Flipside™

Send away for a hardcover by *New York Times* bestselling author Debbie Macomber

How can you get all this?

Buy four Harlequin or Silhouette books during October–December 2003, fill out the form below and send the form and four proofs of purchase (cash register receipts) to the address below.

I accept this amazing offer!
Send me a coupon booklet:

Name (PLEASE PRINT)

Address   Apt. #

City   State/Prov.   Zip/Postal Code

098 KIN DXHT

Please send this form, along with your cash register receipts
as proofs of purchase, to:

In the U.S.:
Harlequin Coupon Booklet Offer, P.O. Box 9071, Buffalo, NY 14269-9071

In Canada:
Harlequin Coupon Booklet Offer, P.O. Box 609, Fort Erie, Ontario L2A 5X3

Allow 4–6 weeks for delivery. Offer expires December 31, 2003.
Offer good only while quantities last.

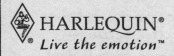

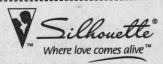

Visit us at www.eHarlequin.com

Q42003

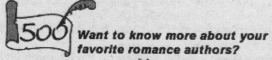

Your opinion is important to us! Please take a few moments to share your thoughts with us about your experiences with Harlequin and Silhouette books. Your comments will be very useful in ensuring that we deliver books you love to read.
Please take a few minutes to complete the questionnaire, then send it to us at the address below.

Send your completed questionnaires to:
Harlequin/Silhouette Reader Survey, P.O. Box 9046, Buffalo, NY 14269-9046

---

1. As you may know, there are many different lines under the Harlequin and Silhouette brands. Each of the lines is listed below. Please check the box that most represents your reading habit for each line.

Line	Currently read this line	Do not read this line	Not sure if I read this line
Harlequin American Romance	❏	❏	❏
Harlequin Duets	❏	❏	❏
Harlequin Romance	❏	❏	❏
Harlequin Historicals	❏	❏	❏
Harlequin Superromance	❏	❏	❏
Harlequin Intrigue	❏	❏	❏
Harlequin Presents	❏	❏	❏
Harlequin Temptation	❏	❏	❏
Harlequin Blaze	❏	❏	❏
Silhouette Special Edition	❏	❏	❏
Silhouette Romance	❏	❏	❏
Silhouette Intimate Moments	❏	❏	❏
Silhouette Desire	❏	❏	❏

2. Which of the following best describes why you bought *this book?* One answer only, please.

the picture on the cover	❏	the title	❏
the author	❏	the line is one I read often	❏
part of a miniseries	❏	saw an ad in another book	❏
saw an ad in a magazine/newsletter	❏	a friend told me about it	❏
I borrowed/was given this book	❏	other: _____	❏

3. Where did you buy *this book?* One answer only, please.

at Barnes & Noble	❏	at a grocery store	❏
at Waldenbooks	❏	at a drugstore	❏
at Borders	❏	on eHarlequin.com Web site	❏
at another bookstore	❏	from another Web site	❏
at Wal-Mart	❏	Harlequin/Silhouette Reader	❏
at Target	❏	Service/through the mail	
at Kmart	❏	used books from anywhere	❏
at another department store or mass merchandiser	❏	I borrowed/was given this book	❏

4. On average, how many Harlequin and Silhouette books do you buy at one time?

I buy _____ books at one time	❏
I rarely buy a book	❏

MRQ403HAR-1A

5. How many times per month do you shop for any *Harlequin and/or Silhouette* books? One answer only, please.

1 or more times a week	❑	a few times per year	❑
1 to 3 times per month	❑	less often than once a year	❑
1 to 2 times every 3 months	❑	never	❑

6. When you think of your ideal heroine, which *one* statement describes her the best? One answer only, please.

She's a woman who is strong-willed	❑	She's a desirable woman	❑
She's a woman who is needed by others	❑	She's a powerful woman	❑
She's a woman who is taken care of	❑	She's a passionate woman	❑
She's an adventurous woman	❑	She's a sensitive woman	❑

7. The following statements describe types or genres of books that you may be interested in reading. Pick *up to 2 types* of books that you are most interested in.

I like to read about truly romantic relationships	❑
I like to read stories that are sexy romances	❑
I like to read romantic comedies	❑
I like to read a romantic mystery/suspense	❑
I like to read about romantic adventures	❑
I like to read romance stories that involve family	❑
I like to read about a romance in times or places that I have never seen	❑
Other: _____	❑

The following questions help us to group your answers with those readers who are similar to you. Your answers will remain confidential.

8. Please record your year of birth below.

19 _____

9. What is your marital status?

single ❑   married ❑   common-law ❑   widowed ❑
divorced/separated ❑

10. Do you have children 18 years of age or younger currently living at home?

yes ❑   no ❑

11. Which of the following best describes your employment status?

employed full-time or part-time ❑   homemaker ❑   student ❑
retired ❑   unemployed ❑

12. Do you have access to the Internet from either home or work?

yes ❑   no ❑

13. Have you ever visited eHarlequin.com?

yes ❑   no ❑

14. What state do you live in?

_____

15. Are you a member of Harlequin/Silhouette Reader Service?

yes ❑   Account # _____   no ❑   MRQ403HAR-1B

If you enjoyed what you just read,
then we've got an offer you can't resist!

Take 2 bestselling love stories FREE!

Plus get a FREE surprise gift!

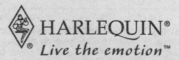